Shades of Truth

Other Books in the Growing Faithgirlz!™ Library

Fiction

From Sadie's Sketchbook

Shades of Truth (Book One)

Flickering Hope (Book Two)

Sophie's World Series

Sophie's World

Sophie's Secret

Sophie Under Pressure

Sophie Steps Up

Sophie's First Dance

Sophie's Stormy Summer

Sophie's Friendship Fiasco

Sophie and the New Girl

Sophie Flakes Out

Sophie Loves Jimmy

Sophie's Drama

Sophie Gets Real

The Girls of Harbor View

Girl Power

Rescue Chelsea

Raising Faith

Secret Admirer

The Lucy Series

Lucy Doesn't Wear Pink (Book One)

Lucy Out of Bounds (Book Two)

Lucy's Perfect Summer (Book Three)

Lucy Finds Her Way (Book Four)

Boarding School Mysteries

Vanished (Book One)

Betrayed (Book Two)

Burned (Book Three)

Poisoned (Book Four)

Nonfiction

My Faithgirlz Journal

The Faithgirlz! Handbook

The Faithgirlz! Cookbook

No Boys Allowed

What's A Girl To Do?

Girlz Rock

Chick Chat

Real Girls of the Bible

Faithgirlz! Whatever!

My Beautiful Daughter

Beauty Lab

Body Talk

Everybody Tells Me to Be Myself,
But I Don't Know Who I Am

Girl Politics

Bibles

The Faithgirlz! Bible

NIV Faithgirlz! Backpack Bible

Faithgirlz! Bible Studies

Secret Power of Love

Secret Power of Joy

Secret Power of Goodness

Secret Power of Modesty

Check out www.faithgirlz.com

From Sadie's Sketchbook

Shades of Truth

Book One

Naomi Kinsman

ZONDER**kidz**

ZONDERVAN.com/
AUTHORTRACKER
follow your favorite authors

ZONDERKIDZ

Shades of Truth
Copyright © 2011 by Naomi Kinsman Downing

This title is also available as a Zondervan ebook.
Visit www.zondervan.com/ebooks

Requests for information should be addressed to:

Zonderkidz, *Grand Rapids, Michigan 49530*

Library of Congress Cataloging-in-Publication Data

Downing, Naomi Kinsman, 1977-
    Shades of truth / Naomi Kinsman Downing.
        p. cm. — (Faithgirlz!) (From Sadie's sketchbook ; bk. 1)
        Summary: When twelve-year-old Sadie has to move away from her home in
    California, she wrestles with questions of faith.
    ISBN 978-0-310-72662-3 (softcover)
    1. Moving, Household—Fiction. 2. Christian life—Fiction. I. Title.
PZ7.D75933Sh 2011
[Fic]—dc23   2011038069

Editor: Kim Childress
Cover design: Cindy Davis
Interior design and composition: Greg Johnson/Textbook Perfect

Printed in the United States of America

---

11 12 13 14 15 /DCI/ 20 19 18 17 16 15 14 13 12 11 10 9 8 7 6 5 4 3 2 1

For my husband, Dave,
who introduced me to the black bears.

Chapter 1

Candlelight

The old-fashioned candleholder made shadows cartwheel across the walls as I tiptoed toward the stacked boxes. My new bedroom was dark. Middle of the forest, middle of the night dark. Dad had promised to turn on the power tomorrow, but for tonight we were eighteenth century — or whenever it was they read by candlelight. The hundred-year-old log cabin creaked and popped. Bullfrogs and crickets sang outside. I'd been in Owl Creek only a few hours, but my life had already become a grand adventure.

The presents waited on top of the pile, each with a card taped to the top. I'd pinky-promised the girls I wouldn't open them until I was alone in my new room, so all day, as I sat in the Jeep's back seat, getting closer and closer to Michigan, I'd thought of nothing else. Now, slowly, so the candle wouldn't flicker out, I carried the four wrapped boxes back to bed. I snuggled under the covers and lined up the presents.

Juliet first.

Sadie,
I can't believe you won't be here for seventh grade. We
will miss, miss, miss you.
xo, Juliet

Deep in the box, she'd buried her top-secret brownie recipe with a note:

No matter what, never, ever share this recipe. Especially
with Pippa. You know she's only my friend for the brownies.

I choked back my laugh, not wanting to wake up my parents.

Alice next.

S—
Remember when we filled Juliet's closet with balloons
for her birthday? Here's some more, just in case.
A

She'd wrapped bags and bags of balloons, enough to fill five closets.

Now Bri.

Sadie,
I had to get these for you. They had Sadie written all over them.
Miss you already, Bri

They were perfect. Purple Pumas with silver laces.

One present left. I picked it up and ran my fingers along the shiny paper. Pippa.

Sades,
Don't cry. I know you won't. I'm sure you're having adventures already. Since you love dragging things out for as long as possible, here's the deal with this present. It's the top ten reasons you'll always be my best friend. Look at the tenth reason now, but save the rest. Look at them one at a time, only when you really need them. And write me. Write me, write me, write me.
x's and o's to infinity, Pips

. I blinked back tears as I turned to the first page of the photo album.

WHY PIPPA REYNOLDS AND SADIE DOUGLAS WILL ALWAYS BE BEST FRIENDS.

REASON 10: WE'VE ALWAYS BEEN THERE FOR EACH OTHER, EVEN WHEN THINGS WERE REALLY, REALLY BAD.

The first picture was Pips on her second birthday, crying as she spit out her cake, because the thick layer of coconut felt like sandpaper against her tongue and ruined the frosting. I sat beside her stabbing the cake with my fork. Pips hates coconut to this day.

In the next picture, we were seven, side by side on a bench in Disneyland, drooping miserably in Mickey Mouse ears. I'd refused to ride Space Mountain because I was scared to go into the dark. Pips stayed with me while our friends rode.

In the last picture, we stood grinning in ski gear, arms around each other. Dad had snapped this photo just before the ski patrol found him, two years ago, when Mom had collapsed on her way down the mountain. She was still sick.

I put the album on my bedside table, feeling full and empty at the same time. One day, Mom sped around, shuttling us to soccer and tucking me into bed before working an eight-hour night shift at the hospital. The next, she could hardly stand up without collapsing. Mom used to be like an armful of fireworks, blasting into a room. Now she was like my candle's flickering flame. People held their breath to keep from accidentally blowing her out.

The cartwheeling shadows had turned into monsters. Their whispers filled the darkness: *Your mom will never get better. No matter what you try, your life is totally out of your control.*

"No," I whispered as I blew out the candle. "You're not allowed here, in our new house, in our new life. Go back to the monster world and leave us alone."

I stared, unseeing, at the ceiling, trying to fall asleep, trying to convince myself tomorrow would be better. It would be, if I had anything to do with it. I would chase all the shadows away.

Chapter 2

Moose Tracks

I woke to the smell of freshly ground coffee, scrambled eggs, and maple syrup. Pale pink sunlight spilled into my room. I threw off my covers and hurried to the window seat, impatient to see the yard, which had been too dark to see in the sliver of moonlight last night. Tall pine trees guarded the house, and instead of grass, a carpet of needles covered the ground. Dad wasn't kidding about living in the forest.

I slipped on my fluffy purple slippers to protect my feet from the ice-cold floorboards and headed downstairs. In the kitchen, Dad stood over the stove in a ruffled pink apron. His sandy blonde hair was doing the usual, every-which-way morning thing.

Around him were dishes, pots, pans, scattered papers, and haphazardly piled boxes, "Sugar, spice, and everything nice?" I asked, reading the embroidery on his apron.

Dad grinned. "Couldn't find anything else, and I couldn't bear to open another box."

I gathered and smoothed paper. Once the kitchen table was clear, I found knives, forks, and plates. "Where are the napkins?"

"Only one way to find out." Dad turned off the burners and dished up three plates. "Think of it as a treasure hunt."

"Yeah, right." I decided to go without.

He piled the pancakes higher and higher on each plate.

"Dad! Mom won't eat that much."

"Wilderness air makes everyone hungry." Dad whipped off the apron with a flourish.

"What are you doing today?" I helped Dad carry the plates to the table. Dad had given up his mediation job in Silicon Valley to find a quieter place for us to live. The Michigan Department of Natural Resources—otherwise known as the DNR—had hired him to help the hunters, the residents, and a bear researcher agree on a way to coexist. According to the stories, they couldn't agree on anything. Today was his first day.

"Off to meet Helen Baxter, the scientist researching the bears. She called this morning and invited me to follow bears around the forest with her."

Halfway to the table, I almost dropped the syrup container. "Is that safe?"

"Helen says the biggest danger is being eaten alive by mosquitoes." Dad turned to the doorway and attempted to smooth his hair. "Ahhh. The princess has awoken. Lured by the coffee?"

From the doorway Mom narrowed her eyes at Dad. "Ha, ha."

He handed her a steaming mug. Mom never was a morning person, even before she got sick. It took at least two cups of coffee before she woke up. Contrary to me and Dad, however, Mom looked perfect in the morning, just like every other time of day. It wasn't fair. I inherited Dad's untamable blond curls and freckles, instead of Mom's silky red layers and china-doll face. At least I had Mom's bright green eyes, but sometimes it's hard to be grateful for the little things.

"Let's eat. I'm starving," I said.

We all sat down and dug in.

Dad cut his pancakes into triangle wedges. "After I go to Helen's, I think I'll go over to the DNR to meet my new boss, Meredith Taylor. She's the ranger for this area. I'd like to take the local temperature before next week's meeting." He looked at me. "Any plans for your last day of freedom? Do you want to come?"

I pictured us, crashing through bushes, swatting mosquitoes, sneaking up on a bear. "Ummm … Maybe I should unpack. You know, before school starts tomorrow." I poured maple syrup onto the exact center of my top pancake until it pooled and spilled over the sides. "Plus I have to write to Pippa and the girls. Then maybe Mom will take me downtown to explore."

I looked at her hopefully, but she still stared into her cup of coffee.

"Well, possibly when she wakes up." Dad elbowed Mom.

She elbowed him back. "We'll see, Sadie."

Already it was a good day. Mom must have slept well last night. Maybe Dad was right. A change of pace, and she'd be better in no time.

I helped clean up breakfast, waved as Dad pulled away in his Jeep, and headed upstairs to unpack.

After a couple hours Mom called, "How's it going, Sadie?"

I went out to the landing, which overlooked the living room with its stone fireplace and thick wooden beams. Mom faced an enormous pile of boxes.

Last night's shadow monsters crept onto my shoulders, crowding my mind with worries. Just settling into our new life would exhaust Mom. I took the stairs two at a time. "Let's go downtown, Mom."

"But there's so much to do here."

"I'm almost finished with my room. I'll help with the rest when we get home." I threw my arms around her. "Come on, please, please, please, please?"

"Oh, all right. Get your coat. It's cold."

The coat was the last thing on my mind. I hurried upstairs, thinking only of my new purple shoes. After stripping out of my dust-streaked clothes, I put on my favorite jeans with the silver-star pattern, and a long-sleeved purple shirt. I soaked my curls and twisted them into two braids, and then I slipped into the shoes. The perfect outfit — Bri would have been proud.

"Sadie!" Mom called.

"Coming!" Still needed a coat. I grabbed my lime-colored ski jacket and shoved my arms into the sleeves.

Mom's car waited for us in the driveway. The moving company had dropped it off when they unloaded our pod, which had been stuffed full of everything that hadn't fit in the Jeep. When we climbed in the car, I noticed Dad had taped an envelope onto the steering wheel.

Mom winked at me. "Mad money."

When I was little, Dad surprised me with mad money tucked under my pillow or into my suitcase. Mad money was strictly for luxuries, never necessities.

On the drive into town, I rolled down the window and let cold air rush through my fingers. Wide-open sky. Clean air tinged with sharp pine. I wanted to spring out of the car—to twirl and shout and dance.

We turned onto Main Street. Rustic wood signs topped the log buildings. Moose Tracks Trading Post. Black Bear Java. A post with wooden arrows pointed toward the library, the Catholic church, and White Pine Academy, my new school.

Mom pulled into a parking spot. When she smiled, the lines around her eyes tightened. "Why don't you take the mad money? I think I'll wait here."

She leaned back against the headrest and closed her eyes. I hated, hated, hated this disease: Chronic Fatigue Syndrome, the doctors diagnosed, after almost a year of tests. Meaning she had exhaustion they couldn't cure—exhaustion that came on like a wave, with no warning, so that Mom sunk deep into herself, hardly able to speak or walk or even smile.

We'd given up on treatments, which only raised our hopes and then failed.

Swallowing disappointment, I opened my door. Next time, Mom and I would explore the shops, searching for funny t-shirt slogans. We'd find the best local chocolate delicacy, and choose postcards to send back home.

Chimes rang as I opened Moose Tracks Trading Post's front doors and breathed in the smell of leather and wood smoke. A girl about my age with white-blonde hair pulled up in a messy knot stood by a bulletin board.

"Hey." I walked over, hoping to make a new friend. "That's my dad's meeting." I pointed to the flyer she was reading. "Are you going?"

The girl turned around, looked me up and down, staring especially at my shoes, and said, "Your dad is Matthew Douglas?"

"Yes." I backed away from the coldness in her voice.

She folded her arms. "So you're out to snoop around? We're not interested in being pushed around by a big shot from California."

I forced a small laugh. "I'm not—My dad isn't—"

The girl leaned forward, her voice sharp as broken glass. "Bears are like rats. They dig in our garbage, eat people's pets, and scare little kids. Thanks to that crazy scientist, Helen, we can't shoot a bear that trespasses on our property unless it's hunting season. And now your dad's here to make everything worse."

I stared at the girl's chipped red fingernail polish and

tried to picture her very ordinary looking hands, hands that could be Bri's or Alice's, holding a gun or maybe even shooting a bear. Back home, no families I knew owned a gun. I'd never even seen a gun in real life, other than behind glass in a museum.

"Ummm." I took a couple steps back.

"What's up, Frankie?" A tall boy wearing an oversized flannel shirt walked over. "Who's this?"

At least I knew her name now.

"This, Ty, is Matthew Douglas's kid checking up on the locals."

Ty's expression hardened. "Give your dad a message for me. The sooner you and your family head out of town, the better."

A gray-haired man joined us, wiping his hands on his jeans. "What's going on?"

"Nothing," Ty said. "Just passing along a message. Come on, Frankie. Let's go."

I watched them leave, trying to match my idea of kids in Owl Creek with the reality of these two. Their anger clung to my skin and echoed in my ears. How could they hate me and my family, without even knowing us?

"You all right?" the man asked.

"Sure. Fine." I walked to the car on shaky legs.

"You didn't spend the mad money," Mom said.

"Maybe next time." I left my window up on the drive home and watched the afternoon shadows stretch long between the trees.

From: Sadie Douglas
To: Pippa Reynolds
Date: Monday, September 1, 9:12 PM
Subject: Do NOT use soap to get tree sap out of your hair

We unpacked today. Mom had OPINIONS about where to hang pictures. :) This new house is good for her. I've already learned important lessons about living in the forest. Like what to do when a woodpecker drills into your wall. And how to get sap out of your hair. Turns out peanut butter is magic. Ha!

Dad saw four bears in the forest today with Helen, the bear scientist. The mother, Patch, didn't like how close Dad was and stomped her paws and huffed at him as her cubs climbed up a tree. He tried to act like he wasn't afraid, but he must have been. He says I can see a bear tomorrow if I want to. Do I want to?

Tell the girls I love my gifts. I'll write them soon. I love, love, love my album and promise not to look at the next page until I really need to.

Chapter 3

White Pine

After the scene at Moose Tracks yesterday, I realized maybe the Pumas were over the top. I tried on white running shoes, but they made my size seven and a half feet look like ocean liners, and last year's shoes were too small. I might as well wear the Pumas.

"Sadie," Dad called. "Jeep's heading out!"

I changed shoes and grabbed my backpack. Dad revved the engine when I slid into my seat.

"Hang on!" He dropped the emergency break.

The tires kicked up gravel as we spun out of the driveway, and Dad made squealing sound-effects as we sped around corners. Wind whipped my hair into my eyes. I knew he wanted to give me back yesterday's excitement. Last night, he noticed something was wrong, but thankfully, because he was Dad, he hadn't forced it out of me. Dad never talked

21

things to death. Instead he'd do something wild like this until I laughed so hard I forgot why I was upset.

When we pulled up to White Pine Academy, Frankie leaned up against the bike rack. She rolled her eyes as Dad squealed one last time. I didn't care. So what if one girl in my new school didn't like me? To be honest, I didn't like her much either.

Moss and vines crept over the school's weatherworn roof and down the gray walls. Odd-shaped windows looked out of three floors of classrooms, with a few tiny, round windows at the tip-top. Maybe a fourth floor attic? A new wing had been built onto the left side of the building, but still it didn't look like enough room for kindergarten through eighth grade. I followed the signs to the main office to get my schedule. The seventh grade classroom was on the third floor, and apparently we stayed in that one room all day, other than for music and gym. Our science teacher, math teacher, and Spanish teacher visited our room—to teach all twenty-four of us.

As I walked to my classroom, I prayed Frankie wasn't one of those twenty-four. Of course, when I walked into my classroom, there she sat, on Ty's desk in the back row, repainting her fingernails. A group of girls crowded around her.

"Frankie, open a window," Ty said. "That stuff stinks."

"I'll do it." A girl with shoulder-length blonde hair and tons of freckles rushed to the window.

Three boys sauntered past me into the classroom, fortunately not giving me a second look. Ty stood to high-five them. "Nick," slap. "Mario," slap. "Demitri," slap.

Ty's friends claimed the other three desks in the back row and wadded up paper, using the girls for target practice, while the girls ducked and hurried for desks of their own.

A woman breezed through the door, glasses askew, carrying a stack of papers and books. As she passed me, the top book clattered to the floor. Another few fell as she reached for the first.

"Can you get those?" She stood and rebalanced her pile. "Oh. You must be Sadie. I'm Ms. Barton."

The room went silent and eyes burned into my back. Perfect. Another awkward introduction. After I handed over the books, I turned, hoping some brilliant greeting would spring to mind. No such luck.

"Sadie's the one I was telling you about," Frankie said. "Her dad is Matthew Douglas, so be careful what you say to her. She might report you to the DNR."

Immediately, the classroom exploded into angry conversation about Dad and Helen and the DNR and next week's community meeting. From what I could hear, most of the seventh grade agreed with Frankie that bears were like rats.

I'd looked forward to my wilderness adventure all summer, and now here I stood, tongue-tied, staring at everyone.

Frankie grinned. "Nice shoes, Sparkie."

"Sadie," Ms. Barton interrupted. "Welcome. Sit anywhere you like. We don't have assigned seats."

I chose a desk, pretending not to hear one of the girls say, "Sparkie's my dog's name."

Everyone burst into laughter.

Okay. No big deal. The best thing was to laugh too. Once they saw I could take a joke, the Sparkie thing would go away.

Another woman walked in. If people were colors and Ms. Barton was electric orange, this woman would be silky indigo. Her jet-black hair hung halfway down her back, and she wore a bell-sleeved, gauzy white shirt, embroidered with bright yellow and purple flowers.

"To your seats," Ms. Barton announced, straightening her glasses.

Desks scraped and bags thudded as everyone settled in. I glanced around the room, hoping to spot at least one girl who hadn't been in Frankie's pack. There was one, an elf-ishly small girl with black hair that curled under at her chin. Two others had pulled their desks together, sharing head-phones and a single iPod.

"Turn it off," Ms. Barton said. "No iPods during school hours."

"But Ms. B," Frankie said, "Abby and Erin can't breathe without their boy-band tunes."

I smiled at the two girls as they unraveled themselves from the iPod, but they both raised their eyebrows blankly at me, as though to say: *What? Don't think we're on your side, just because Frankie picks on us too.*

"Frankie." Ms. Barton tapped a pen against her finger-tips. "I'm sure we don't need to start our school year with another conversation about respect. We'll go over class rules later, but now we have a special guest."

The indigo woman stepped away from the whiteboard, where she had drawn a moon, a circle, a triangle, three wavy lines, a spiral, and a butterfly.

"Vivian Harris, meet our seventh graders. Most of you have probably seen Vivian's art at Black Bear Java. Some of you may have attended her art show at the library last June."

"Oh goody." Sadie heard Frankie whisper. "An art project, just like kindergarten."

What was wrong with her, Sadie wondered. *Why was Frankie so mean?*

After explaining how artists use universal symbols with specific meanings, Vivian pointed to her drawings on the whiteboard. "A circle means unity or wholeness. Three squiggly lines together symbolize water and vitality. Butterflies can symbolize rebirth or new life."

Vivian asked us to choose three symbols and create a pattern that represented our personality and goals for the year.

"Do we have to choose one of those symbols?" the freckled girl asked. "Because none of those represent me. Like, what am I supposed to say ... I resemble water? That makes no sense."

"You could be like water, Nicole," said the elfish girl. "You know, the way a brook is bubbly and—"

"Ms. Barton!" said Nicole. "Did you hear what Ruth said?"

"I didn't mean ..." began Ruth.

Nicole slid down in her chair. "Whatever. I'm not doing this stupid project."

Ms. Barton's eyes filled with panic.

Vivian walked over to Nicole's desk. "Create any symbol you like. I'll help you brainstorm."

Ms. Barton passed out white paper and I started to think. Three symbols. Here was my second chance to introduce myself to the class. I'd start with shoes, to show the girls I could laugh at myself. The colors were perfect: purple was dramatic and playful and silver added the extra splash of shimmer. I couldn't say that, though, so maybe I'd say the shoes were for energy. Everyone liked energetic people.

The shoes were a complicated symbol, so the next should be simple. I drew a circle around them, but it didn't look right. Plus, circles were for unity. Absolutely no way could I say that was my goal.

What *was* my goal?

I wanted an adventure. Mountains symbolized adventure, right? The shoes could be climbing up.

On the side of the mountain, the shoes needed something like ... sunglasses. Throw in a little California. If I were back home, I might talk about glasses as a symbol for seeing, how I wanted to see people clearly. But here, I'd avoid all that. I sketched sunglasses half an inch above my shoes. Together, they looked like a funny, squat person. Good. A little humor never hurt.

"Are we almost finished?" Ms. Barton asked as she walked around the room. She stopped by my desk. "Sadie, this is excellent. Let's start with you."

From: Sadie Douglas
To: Pippa Reynolds
Date: Tuesday, September 2, 3:42 PM
Subject: On your first day of school

1. Do NOT share your art project first. I thought everyone was actually doing the project. Turns out they were either drawing cartoons of Ms. Barton or yours truly, or they didn't plan to share at all.

2. Do NOT poke fun at yourself. It won't help. My funny squat person drawing tanked. And everyone laughed at me.

3. Do NOT bring a banana for lunch. There is no cool way to eat a banana. Tomorrow will be better. Something good happened today, though. An artist named Vivian Harris came to our class and invited me to take art lessons with her. She's a real artist — she used to live in New York and had a studio and everything. Do you think I should?

Thanks for your email. Give Cocoa a kiss for me. Good thing he didn't get your dad's running shoes. Sorry about your slipper. ;) I'm going to look at Reason Nine, Pips. I'll wait longer next time. I promise.

Chapter 4

Dandelion Wishes

I closed my laptop. We'd been so busy unpacking I'd hardly explored the house. I was dying to climb the spiral staircase that led to a trap door in the ceiling. It could be an attic or—I hoped—it could lead to the round porch I'd seen from outside. I grabbed my scrapbook. That porch was the perfect place for Pippa's reason nine. I climbed up and pushed open the door. Yes! Three more stairs led to the fenced-in deck. I hugged the scrapbook tight and leaned over the rail. Deep-green treetops stretched far into the distance.

An alcove, cut into the wall, sheltered a cushioned seat from the wind. Whoever had lived here before us had clearly loved this porch. I climbed onto the seat.

WHY PIPPA REYNOLDS AND SADIE DOUGLAS WILL ALWAYS
BE BEST FRIENDS —

REASON 9: WE LEARNED TOGETHER THAT DANDELION WISHES DO COME TRUE.

We'd made our first dandelion wish when we were five. My Aunt Molly told us if we blew off all the dandelion seeds and really believed, our wish would come true. Pippa's big sister, Andrea, said magic wasn't real, so we decided to prove her wrong. It was hard-to-breathe-hot that day, and we tried to think of the most magical thing possible. We closed our eyes, wished we'd be ice-freezing cold, and blew off every single seed. Minutes later, Mom came outside with swim-suits and towels and swept us away to the unheated com-munity swimming pool. In the picture Pippa had carefully glued in the scrapbook, we huddled in towels, blue-lipped.

Not every single dandelion wish came true, but other pictures in the scrapbook reminded me that important ones had. Pippa and I posed on brand new bikes without training wheels. The two of us holding the soccer trophy—we'd won the division title. Both of us hugging Cocoa, Pippa's choco-late lab. Cocoa took a whole summer of dandelion wishes last year. I'd wanted my own dog, but we'd settled on shar-ing Cocoa. A dog was probably too much for Mom.

A sticky note in the bottom corner read: *Go find a dande-lion, Sades. Make a wish. You know it will come true.*

But what to wish for? I pulled Vivian's card out of my pocket and turned it over and over in my hands. Art lessons? If I could, I'd paint the ocean on a stormy California day. Or Cocoa, stealing pizza off the counter. Or Mom laughing.

What if there weren't dandelions in Michigan?

After dropping off the scrapbook in my bedroom, I headed outside to find out. Sure enough, along the edge of the cabin, grass and weeds grew in a ragged border. I found a perfect white dandelion, picked it, closed my eyes, and blew.

Dad pulled into the driveway and cut the engine. "Sades! Patch is just down the street with her cubs. Want to see them?"

With school and Vivian Harris and the round porch and the possibility of art lessons, I had almost completely forgotten Dad's offer to show me the bears today. I still hadn't answered my own question. Did I want to see a bear?

"Might as well get it over with. You'll see one soon out and about, I'm sure. Over at Helen's today, I saw at least twelve. My favorite is Big Murphy — he's the biggest, and he's constantly eating. He follows Andrew around with sad-puppy eyes while Andrew fills the feeders."

"Andrew?"

"Helen's son. He helps her at the research station." Dad climbed out of the Jeep with bug spray. "Industrial strength, issued by Meredith with a warning never to go into the forest without a full body spray-down."

He sprayed me head-to-toe. "Now listen, Sadie. First of all, you're never to approach a bear on your own. They're wild animals, never forget that. They follow their instincts, which you can't entirely predict. Helen said black bears need two things, safety and food."

Dad put away the bug spray and hiked into the underbrush. I was torn. If I stayed right on his heels, I was less likely to be pounced on by bears sneaking up behind us. But if I stayed further back, I might have time to run if Dad stumbled across a bear ahead.

Dad pushed aside a branch so it wouldn't hit me in the face. "If you don't frighten the bears, and you don't get between them and their berry bushes, you'll be okay."

"Berry bushes? Don't bears eat meat?"

"Helen says black bears are pretty lazy. They'll eat a deer if it is already dead. But they only hunt live animals when they're desperate."

I grabbed hold of Dad's jacket and tripped along right behind him. *Don't think about bears eating you, Sadie. Think about anything else.* Just before Dad had pulled up, I made my dandelion wish. "Dad, can I take art lessons?"

"Since when have you wanted art lessons?" Dad held up a thorny blackberry vine and ducked under.

"This artist, Vivian Harris, came to our class today. She liked my drawing and invited me to take lessons with her. I think I want to."

"Sounds like you had a nice day."

"Well, that was a good part."

"I'll think about the art lessons." Dad clambered over a fallen log and launched into one of his favorite hiking songs. "The other day ..."

"If we sing, the bears will know exactly where we are." Not to mention how embarrassed I would be if anyone from school heard me.

"Exactly. You want the bears to know where you are, so you don't startle them. I already startled Patch with the Jeep, which is why she sent her cubs up a tree. I think she'll stick around until she's sure it's safe to move on."

I sang along with Dad for a few lines until we stepped onto the gravel road. We slowed, and Dad pointed at a bear fifty feet away with a white patch of fur just below her chin—which had to be Patch. My stomach filled with butterflies, and I had to convince my feet to keep moving forward, step after step. Patch stood guard in front of a tree almost directly across from our closest neighbor's house. Her velvet black fur and her strong beauty took my breath away. If only I could touch her, get closer, look into her eyes. She had to be the biggest, most gorgeous animal I had ever seen outside the zoo. Above, one adorable cub dangled a paw from his perch on a thick branch. Tiny, sharp claws stuck out just beyond his paw pads. A snout poked around the trunk a little further up, quickly followed by the rest of the second cub. The third cub tight-roped on a thick branch, swinging back and forth.

"Hey, bear." Dad stopped twenty feet from Patch. "It's good to give them plenty of room."

"Aren't mother bears supposed to be fierce?"

"Protective, yes," Dad said. "But Helen assures me that black bears won't attack unless they are seriously provoked."

Across the street, a man came out of the house. I was about to wave hi when a gunshot rang out. Dad pulled me close. Patch scrabbled up the tree.

The man muttered under his breath then ratcheted his shotgun, readying to fire again.

"What are you doing?" Dad demanded.

The man took aim. "Don't worry. I'm not going to shoot you."

"Beside the fact you could have hit me or my daughter, it's not hunting season yet." Dad crossed to the middle of the street. "You can't shoot any bears until September tenth. And if you look, it's obvious the bear you're aiming at has a research collar, so out of conscience you shouldn't shoot her even during hunting season. Also, the bear is with cubs. It's illegal to shoot mother bears with cubs. You should know all this."

The man lowered his shotgun. "I'm shooting to scare her, Mr. Matthew Douglas."

"How do you know my name?" Dad asked.

"Everybody knows your meddling name. I'm Jim Paulson, and it's my misfortune to be your neighbor." He smirked at my shoes. "And here's the famous Sadie. My daughter, Frankie, has told me all about you."

I sent desperate signals to Dad. *Come on, Dad, time to go home.*

Frankie's dad leaned over the fence and scowled. "Around here, everyone minds their own business. You have no right to be snooping around my property. Understand?"

Dad put his arm around my shoulders. "We didn't mean to offend. Just watching the bears."

"Watch the bears on your own property." Frankie's dad spat on the ground and stalked away.

Dad and I stood speechless for a full two minutes before we started home. Patch and her cubs had long since run down the tree and into the forest.

"So," Dad said. "I'm the meddling Matthew Douglas.

Doesn't look like I'll be invited on his next hunting trip, huh?"

I stared at Dad in horror. "You couldn't shoot …"

"Well, not Patch, or any of the research bears, that's for sure. And probably not any bear, to tell you the truth. But hunting is important to the ecosystem, Sadie. Meredith tells me when too many bears, deer, and other animals live in the same community, some starve to death in the winter. Besides, I'm not here to stop hunting. You know that."

On the drive to Michigan, we had talked about mediating, about staying neutral, about Dad's job in this community. But Dad wasn't anything like shotgun wielding Jim Paulson. I couldn't picture Dad stalking through the forest, shooting an animal, a beautiful, living animal. The thought made me nauseous. I dodged vines and followed the path Dad picked through the underbrush, but I couldn't think of a single thing to say. Dad seemed caught up in his own thoughts too.

Finally, when we reached our front steps, he smiled sadly at me. "Sorry that wasn't what I expected for your first glimpse of the bears, but I'm glad you saw them anyway." He opened the door, but stopped before going inside. "And I've made up my mind. Sign up for those art lessons."

From: Sadie Douglas
To: Pippa Reynolds
Date: Tuesday, September 2, 9:22 PM
Subject: Baked Rigatoni and Top Secret Brownies

Seriously? Ten pages? What are you supposed to do, stay up all night doing math? Bummer.

Mom made rigatoni for dinner tonight the way she used to and sang "Pizza Pie" at the top of her lungs. After dinner, Dad took me to town to spend my mad money—it's a v. long story—but anyway I got all the ingredients for Juliet's top-secret brownies. More about that in the next email.

I found a dandelion. And Dad said I could take art lessons. Should I have wished for Mom to get better? I'm just afraid that's not the way dandelion wishes work.

Miss you.

From: Sadie Douglas
To: Pippa Reynolds, Juliet Chance, Alice Cheng, Brianna Ingles
Date: Tuesday, September 2, 9:29 PM
Subject: Hi from Michigan

Hi girls,

I miss you tons! Thanks for the presents. I made Juliet's top-secret brownies tonight, and they were much EASIER than I ex-pected. But I WON'T say any more. See, Juliet? You can trust me! Dad took me into the woods tonight and I saw bear cubs. Their ears looked as fuzzy as Cocoa's. I think I'm going to like it here.

x's and o's,
Sadie

Chapter 5

Seeing Shapes

I adjusted my backpack as I walked down the hall, preparing for Frankie and her friends. My second day at the school. All I had to do was get through the day. Afterward, I had my first art lesson with Vivian.

The elfish girl, Ruth, stopped me before I reached the classroom. "Hey. I liked your project. I'm sorry Frankie and Co. were horrible about it. I wanted to talk to you at lunch yesterday, but Ms. Barton made me eat in the classroom and catch up on a test."

I blinked at Ruth, taken completely by surprise. "Frankie and Co.?"

"Speaking of …" Ruth raised her eyebrow, causing me to turn.

Frankie breezed past with Nicole and Tess. "Careful, Ruth. Sparkie might give you fleas."

Ruth waited for the door to shut. "Last year, I was new. My dad is a pastor, so they teased me too."

"Well . . ." I tried to shrug it off. "So your dad is a pastor?"

"Yeah. Our church is a few miles out of town. People from Owl Creek come, but we've got more from Eagle's Nest and Hiawatha."

"We used to go to church. Not much, I guess — just Christmas and Easter. Since your dad's the pastor, do you have to go every week?"

"Something like that." Ruth laughed. "Don't look so shocked."

She held the door for Ms. Barton, who had walked over balancing her usual pile of papers and books.

"Planning to come to class today, girls?"

"Yes," we said in unison.

Ruth caught my arm. "I have to go to the dentist today, but tomorrow, want to go for ice cream?" When I hesitated, she added, "Black Bear Java has sixty-two flavors."

I couldn't help smiling. "Sure."

Fortunately, Ms. Barton didn't have any share-your-soul art projects in store for us. We spent most of the day at our desks, studying light and sound waves, algebra, and poetry. When we did get out of the classroom for lunch and PE, Ruth had already gone. I felt split in two. Half of me — California Sadie, the ringleader who organized the parties, who launched the adventures, who didn't care what anyone thought — coolly observed Frankie's jabs and taunts. The other half — Michigan Sadie — felt each word's sting. By the end of the day, I felt bruised and battered as though I'd suffered a wrestling match.

Dad had dropped off my bike so I could ride to Vivian's house. Mom was supposedly resting at home, but more likely, she was climbing up the walls. Of all the doctor's advice, the worst was, "*Take it easy*." Lying around never made Mom feel better; instead, it made her depressed. The only thing worse than being sick with a disease doctors couldn't treat, was being sick *and* depressed.

The ride to Vivian's took me through town and up a one-lane road. Almost as soon as I turned off Main Street, I plunged into the forest. A wooden sign carved with the name *Harris* marked Vivian's gravel driveway. Cement sculptures covered with glossy ceramic shards peeked through the forest surrounding the driveway.

The front of Vivian's house was one enormous floor-to-ceiling window, with a wrap-around porch and a swing hanging next to the door.

"Can I help you?" A man's voice startled me.

I spun around. "I'm sorry. I'm looking for Vivian—for art lessons. I suppose I could knock, but I hadn't gotten to the front door yet since I was admiring the view."

"Whoa, whoa, whoa!" The man held up his armful of branches. "I was out collecting kindling. I didn't mean to surprise you. I'm Vivian's son, Peter."

I smiled, feeling more like myself than I had all day. "I'm Sadie."

"This way." When Peter opened the front door, the smell

of lavender and baking cookies wafted out. "She always bakes when she's excited about a new project."

As I stepped into the entryway, I stopped, stunned by the enormous canvases that covered the log walls. The painting to my right was of a lemon yellow and mandarin orange sunset above the ocean. To my left, a wall-sized fish tank swarmed with bright tropical fish. Four abstract paintings in shades of red hung on the wall behind the tank.

"Mom!" Peter called.

Vivian bustled around the corner in a zebra-striped apron, her nose streaked with flour.

"Sadie. You're here!" She wiped her face. "We'll paint in the blue room."

Peter smiled at me. "A rare treat. Not many people visit the blue room."

"Oh posh. Go away and let us work."

"Save me a cookie," Peter said.

I couldn't help liking Peter, particularly because I had been nervous about art lessons. Vivian had surprised me when she told me I had skill, and now I wanted her words to be true, so much that I nearly ran two stop signs on my bike ride over. Peter had set me at ease. Vivian loaded a tray with cookies and led me through the house into a sunroom art studio. Through the glass ceiling and walls, the woods beckoned. She'd painted the one wooden wall indigo and dotted it with galaxies of stars.

"They glow in the dark," Vivian said, apologetically. "Sometimes I get carried away and act like I'm six. Peter's right, I keep this room secret. I say it's because of the clutter, but really it's the stars. Most people wouldn't understand."

"I used to have glow in the dark stars on my ceiling," I said.

"When you were little, right? Well, they say the older you get, the younger you are at heart." Vivian chose a stool at the wide, paint-flecked table. "Have a cookie."

Butter and sugar melted on my tongue, with hints of almond and lavender. I felt like I'd slipped into another world, of tropical fish, exotic spices, and color-coded rooms.

"Now we'll start." She handed me a blank sketchbook and charcoal pencils.

My palms went clammy as my earlier fears returned. I couldn't draw. I mean, I could doodle, but those charcoal pencils looked like serious art tools.

"I'm not really sure . . ." I began.

"We'll start with shape and proportion." Vivian set a clump of grapes on the table. "If you really look at any object, you'll see it's made of very basic shapes. A circle, oval, square, rectangle, or a triangle. Maybe it is a combination. Drawing isn't about your hand and a pencil. Drawing is about seeing."

She took out her own sketchbook. "Time to draw."

"But I don't know how." I felt dumb. She'd just said drawing was easy, but the clump of grapes wasn't any one basic shape.

Vivian looked up, her pencil mid-stroke. "What shape do you see?"

"The grapes are ovals. But I don't know how to make them look right together."

40

"Excellent." She traced a group of three ovals. "You're talking about proportion — the relationship between objects. A clump of grapes is a bunch of ovals, but what is the overall shape?"

"A ... triangle?"

"What do you need a teacher for?" Vivian added a light triangle to her page. "Start by sketching the triangle, and then draw all the grapes inside."

I started to sketch. Thankfully, Vivian was busy on her own drawing, so I felt less like a fish in her tank. When I put my pencil down, Vivian wiped charcoal off her hands and handed me a rag to do the same. My grapes looked remarkably like the real clump, if a little flat.

"Its not as hard as I thought," I said. "Just drawing ovals and triangles."

"The first step is learning to see. Most people go through their whole lives seeing exactly what they expect, for instance, that grapes are little ovals. But when you look carefully, you see that each grape is a unique oval, slightly different from every other."

I held my drawing at arms-length. "My grapes do look a little flat."

Vivian looked over my shoulder. "We'll talk about perspective next time. In the meantime, don't worry about flat. Practice seeing shapes, and sketch every day. Want a cookie for the road?"

Chapter 6

Running Circles

"**M**om!" The screen door banged shut behind me.

No answer. I looked around the living room, the kitchen, the backyard. She must be upstairs. I pushed their bedroom door open a crack. The curtains were pulled—never a good sign. She lay on the bed, eyes closed, her lips silently moving.

"Mom?" I whispered.

"Sadie." Mom sat up too quickly and pressed her palm to her forehead. "I didn't know you were home."

"What were you doing?"

"Don't be worried, sweetheart. I was just ... praying."

As far as I knew, Mom never prayed outside of church. "Are you okay?"

"Does it have to be a tragedy for a mom to pray now and then?" She rubbed her temples. "Sadie ..."

I sat next to her on the bed. Some days were worse than others, the worst being the days she stopped believing she'd get better.

"Mom, of course you can pray. Whatever you need to do."

"No, you're right. Why would God listen to me now? I've said all of three prayers in my life."

"I didn't mean ..."

"I'm just so tired, Sades. And the more I lay around, the more tired I get."

"Give our new life a chance, Mom." My words sounded hollow, even to me.

Still, Mom pretended to smile. We had played this game ever since she first got sick—both of us pretending that we'd send the monsters away by ignoring them.

"So how was school? How was art?"

"I drew grapes. And I made a friend." There. No need to give her all the details and depress her even more.

Mom tried to stand but her legs buckled. I leapt off the bed and caught her. Her shoulders were skin and bones.

"Lay down, Mom. I can make spaghetti for dinner. Would you like a glass of water?"

Mom leaned back against the pillows. "That would be lovely." She caught my hand, her skin soft as rose petals. "Thank you, Sadie."

When she closed her eyes, I whispered under my breath. "One ... two ... three ..." By the time I'd counted to fifty, her expression smoothed and her breathing calmed. She would be all right. I filled her glass, closed the door quietly, and went downstairs to boil water.

Look at what's real, Sadie, not at what you expect. What did I expect? That Mom would get better no matter what? And God? If he hadn't helped already, why would he help now?

"Sadie, Sadie, Sades!" Dad blasted through the front door and into the kitchen.

He picked me up, swung me around, and breathed in deep. "Smells heavenly."

"You should check on Mom," I kept my voice as light as I dared. "The spaghetti will be done in a few minutes."

"Spaghetti Sadie-style. Love it."

His footsteps echoed up the stairs, and soon his voice murmured in their room.

I took my time draining the water, letting the steam tickle my nose. Dad came back into the kitchen just as I started spooning noodles onto plates.

"I'll take spaghetti up to Mom later. Let's you and I eat in the kitchen." Dad took his plate. He gave me a tight smile, but his eyes looked grim.

This was how we talked — in big looping circles. He was telling me Mom was okay, for now. The *for now* lodged in my mind, a jagged splinter of memories of Mom's bad days, weeks, sometimes even months. When the exhaustion settled in, no one knew how long it would remain. No one knew how long we'd tell ourselves Mom was okay. As though okay was enough. Suddenly, I needed tomorrow to be different. Tomorrow I had to escape the house, if only for a few hours, just so I could breathe.

"Can I get ice cream after school tomorrow with Ruth?"

"Who's Ruth?"

As we ate, I told him about Ruth and then about Vivian's house, the cookies, the fish, the paintings, and her art studio. By the time I finished describing my drawing of the grapes, I was grinning.

Dad put down his fork. "Sadie, this calls for a celebration. Let's go into town and get marshmallows. Mom might even help us toast s'mores in the fireplace."

We sang along to the country station all the way into town. Murray's grocery store was a long building at the end of Main Street. We bought marshmallows and graham crackers and mini-chocolate bars and then piled back into the Jeep. On our way home, just after we'd crossed the bridge, a shot echoed through the forest, followed by a low bellow. Dad slowed, looking into the trees. He pulled onto the shoulder and left the Jeep running.

"Stay in the car, Sadie."

I couldn't just sit there. When Dad cleared the tree line, I turned off the car, jumped down and followed. I found him a little way in, squinting into the trees, listening.

My heart thudded, and I was too afraid to keep from asking, "What?"

"Sadie, you shouldn't be here. This is really dangerous."

Another bellow, closer now, just to our left.

I gasped, "Was that a bear?" At that moment a red-brown

bear burst out of the bushes a few feet in front of us. His back leg bled freely, and he held it at an awkward angle as he crashed past. I couldn't breathe. I grabbed onto Dad, my heart beating like a hammer strike in my ears, behind my eyes, in my throat.

"Let's go." Dad pulled me toward the Jeep.

I wanted to run away, to hide from the bear and the gunner too, but the bear's leg hanging useless tugged at my memory, reminding me of Cocoa's leap from the top level of Pippa's play structure. Just a puppy, he'd shattered his leg, but instead of letting us help him he had run, frenzied with fear and pain. "Shouldn't we help the bear?"

"Helen will know what to do. Come on. And Meredith will want to know too."

When we were almost out of the trees, Dad threw out his arm, holding me back. A dented black ATV bounced onto the road. We saw only the back of the driver's head, his orange vest, and green fishing hat with a red feather. We waited until he'd passed and then sprinted for the Jeep.

Not fast enough. By the time we'd pulled back onto the highway, the ATV was gone.

"That was Jim Paulson, wasn't it, Dad? He had that vest on the other night."

"Lots of people could have that same vest."

"But he was hunting, wasn't he? It's not September tenth yet."

"Correct." We pulled up to a red light, and when Dad looked over at me, the corners of his mouth were white, "Big Murphy."

"What?"

"I don't think that was just any bear, Sades. That was Big Murphy."

Dad's favorite. Hunting season hadn't started yet, and already bears were getting hurt. "I hate this."

"Me too." The light turned green, and our tires screeched as Dad accelerated too fast.

"Then tell someone Jim is out shooting bears when he isn't supposed to be. Isn't keeping the law your job?"

"I will tell Meredith about Big Murphy. I'm just not sure it was Jim ..."

"Dad!"

"Enough, Sadie." He turned into our driveway. "I have to call Helen and Meredith."

From: Sadie Douglas
To: Pippa Reynolds
Date: September 3, 2010, 8:10 PM
Subject: Is praying like wishing?

I found Mom praying today. Mom never prays. Maybe she prays more than I realized. Maybe everyone prays all the time, and I just didn't know.

Wishing Mom would get better seems too big for a dandelion. Maybe that's what praying is for. But if there really is a God, a real God, not like a leprechaun or something you believe in when you're little, that God would be so beyond everything, so untouchable, why would He listen to my problems? I'm just one person in a very big world. What if He didn't answer?

Today was awful. On top of Mom having one of her bad days, Dad's favorite bear, Big Murphy, got shot. We think he's not dead, just hurt. Dad called Helen, and she said she'd track Big Murphy to see if she can help.

The ranger, Meredith, is going to ask the hunters if anyone knows what happened. I doubt Jim, the hunter I KNOW did it, will confess.

Pips, I don't want any of the bears to die. And soon, hunters will be out shooting every day. I think maybe I could pray about Big Murphy. And Mom. I think I'll try.

Chapter 7

What You See

Ruth and I studied the case of ice cream tubs. Double
fudge. Peanut butter cup. Licorice.

"Vanilla, please," Ruth said.

"Vanilla?" Was she crazy?

Ruth shrugged. "Vanilla is my favorite."

I finally decided on peanut butter cup and joined Ruth
at a back booth.

"My teeth still hurt from the dentist." Ruth licked her
spoon clean.

She sat up suddenly and blushed bright red.

"What?" I asked.

"Nothing." She shoved another spoonful of ice cream
into her mouth. "Mmmm!"

"Ruth, don't you dare change the subject!"

"Shush!" She jabbed at her ice cream with her spoon.
"He'll hear you."

"Who?" I glanced over my shoulder.

"Don't look!"

"If you'd tell me, I wouldn't have to."

"Fine," she snapped. "It's Cameron. He's a grade above us—"

"Which one is he?"

"He's wearing a green T-shirt and jeans, and he's just about to ... yeah." Her foot stopped twitching. "He just went through the door."

I turned in time to see the back of Cameron's head.

"Hey, girls." Frankie leaned against the counter next to us, catching me off guard. "It's the flea-bag friends, out enjoying an afternoon on the town."

"Mind your own business, Frankie," Ruth said.

"I warned you about Sparkie's fleas. Too late now." She gave us a signature smirk before calling to Ty, "Hey, wait up."

I watched her go, not hungry for the last few bites of my ice cream. "I'm sorry, Ruth."

"Don't be," she said, eating her last bite of ice cream with a flourish. "And don't let her ruin your ice cream. Frankie thinks she can bully anyone into doing what she wants. I like frustrating her."

I picked my spoon back up. "You don't mind that she teases you?"

"Come on, Sadie. The fleas thing will get old really quickly. What will she tease you about then? You're funny and smart and a good friend. I'm glad I was first to discover you. Soon everyone will turn on Frankie just to get a chance to hang out with you. Don't take her so seriously."

I doubted everything would work out so easily, but I couldn't help smiling. Ruth reminded me a little of Pippa. "So tell me about Cameron." I scooped up the last of my ice cream.

"He plays guitar." Ruth fidgeted with the pearl that hung on her thin gold chain. "He and a couple guys started a band called Equilibrium. They play at the Tree House most Thursdays."

"The Tree House?" We got up, threw away our trash, and started walking back to school. Ruth's mom was going to drive me home.

"Our youth group. We meet every Thursday in a tree house."

We rounded a corner and Ruth said, "Hold up."

She nodded toward a group of kids sitting on the lower roof at the back of the school. We inched behind the bushes.

Ty was telling Nick and Mario a joke, punctuated by Frankie's sharp laughter. Demitri flicked a lighter on and off, scaring Nicole and Tess. He set the corner of a newspaper on fire and then blew it out.

"Last year, someone started a fire back here in a garbage can," Ruth said. "Everyone blamed Ty, but no one could prove it."

Demitri held his lighter too close to Nicole's hair. She shrieked and jumped away.

"The school could have burned down," Ruth said.

"Let's go around the other way. With everything else I'm being accused of, I don't need anyone thinking I'm a snoop."

"Should we tell?" Ruth asked.

Landing Frankie in trouble was tempting, but giving her a reason to hate me would only make things worse. Deep down, even though I doubted it, I hoped Ruth was right and the fleas thing would fade away.

"No," I said. "Promise me you won't, Ruth."

"Okay ..." She didn't sound very sure.

We tiptoed back to the sidewalk and went around to the front of the school. Her mom wasn't there yet, so we sat on the curb. I twisted the seam of my jeans, awkward in the sudden silence. Until I had forced Ruth to make this promise, our new friendship had felt like the two of us against the world. Still, I knew so little about Ruth. Would she keep her promise? I didn't want the afternoon to end this way, with the uncomfortable quiet growing between us. I settled on the one topic I knew Ruth couldn't ignore: Cameron.

"So ... will you see Cameron at youth group tonight? Since it's Thursday?"

Ruth bit her lip, but she couldn't quite hide her smile. "Yes. Our group is going on a mud hike tonight. Penny— she's one of the leaders—takes us on a crazy adventure the first Thursday of each month."

As the tension slid away, I couldn't hide my smile, or my relief either. "A mud hike?"

"Yeah. Who knows what that means. But I'm bringing my boots, for sure. Cameron is playing next week. You want to come hear him?"

I wanted to see the Tree House. And I wanted to hear

Cameron play. It was out of town, so maybe people wouldn't know me—and hate me—already. More importantly, I'd just discovered, when I felt the possibility slipping away, how much I wanted to be Ruth's friend. Ruth's real friend.

I'd never been to a youth group. How bad could it be? "Sure, why not."

Ruth's mom pulled up to the curb. Two red-headed kids, both about six, bounced in the back seat.

"Meet Hannah and Mark, the terrible twins." Ruth reached in the window, ruffled their hair, and then smiled at me. "You'll want to sit up front."

From: Sadie Douglas
To: Pippa Reynolds
Date: Thursday, September 4, 9:23 PM
Subject: Re: Is praying like wishing?

Yes! Praying IS scary. Like finally admitting your tooth really hurts and going to the dentist to find out if you need a filling. If you don't, you're glad you went, but if the news is bad … ;)

That's why I'm afraid to pray about Mom.

Pippa, something weird happened today. Last night, I prayed for Big Murphy. I didn't know what to say, so I just whispered, God, please don't let Big Murphy die, and afterward I felt better. I have no idea why. And today, my new friend Ruth invited me to church. Do you think it's a coincidence?

From: Sadie Douglas
To: Pippa Reynolds
Date: Friday, September 5, 9:15 PM
Subject: Big Murphy

Helen found Big Murphy today!!! He's not radio collared, so it wasn't easy. But when she was out deep in the woods following Humphrey — that's her favorite bear, who she bottle fed when he was an orphan and helped back into the wild — she heard twigs snapping. Big Murphy was rolling in a pile of needles. He wouldn't let her near his leg, but he looked energetic. While she was there, he grazed the nearby blueberry bushes. Helen said those were both great signs. Energy and eating. She thinks if he finds a safe place to hibernate, he'll be okay.

Oh, and Pips ... Dad bought a gun today. He locked it in a safe, but I think he's planning to go out hunting. He says small game hunting, not bear hunting. But Dad, hunting? Doesn't that seem like he's taking this staying neutral thing too far? He tried to make me feel better by offering to take me to the research station tomorrow. More bears. Wish me luck.

Wish you were here.

Chapter 8

And What You Don't

Dad turned into Helen's driveway. "You won't believe the research station, Sadie."

On the long drive from town, over twenty or so miles of bumpy gravel roads, Dad tried to convince me not to be afraid. Still, my heart skipped every third beat. He seemed to think the more he talked, the better I'd feel. "Patch is there with her cubs and a few others," he said.

"Not Big Murphy."

"No. He'll hide out until he's healed a bit. Helen believes he can make it through this, Sades. He's a big, strong bear."

"How does Helen get bears to come to her cabin?" I asked.

"Feeding stations. She's researching alternative feeding when natural food is scarce. So far she's learned bears first eat what they find in the wild. If there isn't enough, they eat nuts and seeds from safe places, like the research station. It's only when both those food sources are missing that bears tear into trash or break into cabins."

My heart stopped beating altogether.

"You okay?" Dad asked.

"Sure. No problem." I reminded myself how beautiful Patch had been. Nothing that beautiful would attack, right? At least if I kept my distance.

"Sades, don't worry. All you'll see today is a bunch of bears hunkered down in feeders."

We pulled up to a two story cabin tucked into a grove of pine trees. The yard crawled with bears. Patch stood beneath a tree, her three cubs balanced on various branches above, peeking down.

A woman bounded out the research station's front door wearing a floppy olive hat, black tank top, and olive pants with at least twelve zippered pockets.

"This must be Sadie!"

"Hi, Helen," Dad said. "Sadie isn't sure whether to leave the safety of the Jeep."

Helen laughed and came over to my door. "I just got back from walking with Humphrey."

Helen helped me down and walked me straight past the bears, over to the wooden porch.

"Bears care about two things." She sat and motioned to the space beside her. A huge bear lumbered across the deck toward a window box filled with seeds. "Safety and food, because they eat all their food in half the year to prepare for hibernation. Most of the time, bears ignore people. Unless, of course, we have food."

"Dad tells me they aren't dangerous." I pushed my back against the wall trying to keep my eye on all the bears at once.

"Actually, I said that bears are wild animals," Dad said. "But they prefer nuts and berries to Sadie-burgers."

I rolled my eyes at Dad. "Not funny."

Helen took off her hat and looked me straight in the eyes. "The bears are familiar with their surroundings, so here, even more than in the wild, they are unlikely to get spooked and react. But in general, black bears are peaceful creatures. I walk through the forest with Humphrey. And I've even approached bears I don't know. But I've studied bears for years. I know their body language. I know when they're anxious."

"But you should never try that yourself," Dad told me.

"No," Helen agreed. "I am very, very careful when I'm out there."

The screen door creaked and a boy about my age with deep, tan skin and a crooked half smile walked onto the deck.

"Hey there."

"Sadie, this is Andrew," Helen said.

Why hadn't anyone told me Helen's son was my age? Why didn't he go to White Pine? If my heart raced any faster, would it explode? My thousand questions must have been all over my face, because Andrew's half smile widened into a grin.

"Thought you'd met everyone around here? How do you like White Pine?"

Helen spoke up. "You'll find Andrew has strong opinions about that school."

"It was just a pudding fight," Andrew said.

Helen shook her head. "It was three." She looked back at me, and I could see she wasn't upset with him. "Andrew has more of a temper than is good for him. In fact, the principal respectfully asked if he might like to be homeschooled."

Andrew shrugged. "Works for me. Chocolate stains are hard to clean off tennis shoes."

"Andrew, could you fill the feeders?" Helen asked. Then she turned to Dad. "Would you look over my presentation for Tuesday's meeting at the DNR?"

Dad followed Helen inside, and Andrew took off for the garage, leaving me sitting on the bench surrounded by bears. It smelled a bit like the zoo, but also like pine and forest. The biggest bear in the yard ambled toward the deck, lazily tilting his head from side to side to keep flies from landing on his ears. His fur was thick and coarse, a deep midnight black. He might be the tiniest bit too close, too.

"That's Yogi. He's looking at me, not you," Andrew said as he walked back across the yard. "Actually, he's looking at the seed bag. Don't worry."

Right. Don't worry. "How much does he weigh?"

"I don't know. Six hundred, seven hundred pounds?"

"And I'm not supposed to worry?"

Andrew slung the bag over his shoulder and rounded the corner of the cabin. "They can smell your fear. Try to relax."

Perfect. I was supposed to relax now? I breathed in. Breathed out. A bear crossed another's path, and they huffed at one another. Nope. I wasn't going to sit here alone. I edged around the cabin.

Andrew topped off one windowsill feeder and went to the next. I counted bears. One scratching his back on the tree. Yogi, stalking Andrew. The two over by the blueberry bushes who hadn't liked one another. Patch and her three cubs. Two small bears on their hind paws eating out of wooden boxes at the edge of the lawn. And one climbing into the scale. That made eleven. Eleven bears against Andrew and me. Would we make the evening news?

"So, have they been giving you a hard time?" Andrew moved on to the next feeder, and I backed along the cabin wall, keeping as many bears in sight as I could.

"You mean at school?"

He looked at me like "Could it be anything else?" It was a friendly expression though.

"Well, Frankie ..." Yogi moved closer and suddenly my throat was too dry to get another word out.

"Hey." Andrew dropped his teasing smile. "I'm sorry. Really, there's nothing to be scared of. I promise."

I nodded, but still couldn't speak. This time I wasn't sure if my problem was Andrew or the bears.

"One more feeder and then I'll show you the creek. Give you a break from the bears, okay?"

He filled the last feeder and threw the empty bag onto the front porch. Fortunately, the path to the creek was at the back of the cabin, away from the feeders and the bears. Unfortunately, to walk down the path, I had to turn my back on them.

"Frankie started the first food fight," Andrew said. "We moved here when I was in third grade. Mom had been working with bears in Yosemite, but then she got a grant to study bear feeding patterns in communities where humans and bears live together. Frankie despised me the minute she met me."

I could finally hear over the pounding in my ears. "Why does she hate everyone?"

"With Frankie, anger is a family trait. And Mom had ideas about how hunting and wildlife laws should change. People don't like change, and no one likes new laws, particularly when they cramp their style."

We turned a corner, and the path dead-ended at a creek.

"Have you ever played Sink the Boat?" Andrew asked.

"What's that?"

"Get some rocks and wait here." He crashed upstream through the bushes.

I gathered a handful of rocks, wondering what Andrew could be up to.

When he returned he held up a stick. "So I toss this in, and we throw our rocks, trying to sink it."

"The stick's the boat?"

"Yep," Andrew said, his crooked smile back.

He flung the stick into the water and we hurled rocks. Even when we hit it, the stick danced away, so Andrew resorted to throwing handfuls of rocks, nearly tackling me any time I stole from his supply. By our third boat, we were laughing so hard we could hardly throw.

"Sadie?" Dad called.

"Down here, Dad," I answered.

Andrew and I each threw a final rock and then raced back up to the cabin. He stopped me before we got to the yard.

"Probably best not to run around the bears."

"Right." The game and the laughing had calmed me down. My heart didn't race as I walked past the bears who ate, nuzzling furry snouts into their feeders. They were beautiful, truly. How could Frankie call them rats? I stopped, not too close, but close enough to examine the nearest bear's snout. What shape was it? Triangle, and square on the end. I pulled out my sketchbook as soon as I buckled myself into the Jeep.

"Next time I *will* sink the boat!" I called to Andrew as we pulled away.

From: Sadie Douglas
To: Pippa Reynolds
Date: Saturday, September 6, 7:45 PM
Subject: Bears everywhere. And Andrew.

I met Helen's son, Andrew—turns out he's our age, but unfortunately, he home schools. I think that means he mostly works with his mom and calls it science. I wish I could do that too. Ha, ha!

I think I like the bears, Pip. I was scared, but I also wanted to touch one. Bear hunting season starts in four days, and I'm worried. I might try praying again tonight for Big Murphy, for all the bears. Is that crazy?

From: Sadie Douglas
To: Pippa Reynolds
Date: Sunday, September 7, 8:22 PM
Subject: Bugs!

People told me to watch out for mosquitoes and for ticks. I should have listened. I am one enormous mosquito bite, and I am covered head to toe in itch cream. Tonight at dinner a tick crawled up my arm. Dad took it off me and said I was lucky it hadn't dug under my skin. Ick.

All this because I went in the forest today with Dad looking for bears. After we tramped through bushes and waded through a stream until my feet practically fell off from overuse, we found bear hair caught in the bark of a tree. And that was it. We could have seen tons of bears at the cabin. But Dad said it's much more spectacular to see bears in the forest???

It's okay, because I'm not ready to see Andrew again yet. And yes, he's nice. Yes, he's cute. But I prefer a friend more than a crush right now. Does that make any sense at all?

From: Sadie Douglas
To: Pippa Reynolds
Date: Monday, September 8, 9:10 PM
Subject: Mosquito bites don't look anything like zits

But Frankie still called me Zitzie all day. I guess the Sparkie thing DID wear out. But Zitzie is worse. :(Probably Frankie just wanted to get in some extra digs before Dad's meeting tomorrow night. Dad asked a group of small game hunters if he could tag along with them today, but fortunately they said no. Dad seemed discouraged about it, though. He's not a hunter. Why is he trying to act like he is one?

And WHY does everyone tell you not to scratch? As though you can help it.

Helen saw Big Murphy again today and he's still looking healthy. Hunting season starts in two days, on Wednesday.

Chapter 9

Jagged Edges

Mom and I got to the meeting late. People already filled the long benches facing the presentation area of the ranger station, but Ruth and her dad saved Mom and I folding chairs at the back of the room. Ruth's mom must be home with the twins. I tried not to look at glass cases that lined the walls, filled with stuffed beavers, raccoons, and rabbits, or, worst of all, the moose head mounted on a plaque above Dad's podium.

"Most of us love living in the wild among wild creatures," Dad was saying. "And we also know that living side by side requires particular care."

Ruth leaned over to whisper, "All of this, under a dead moose's head."

I choked back my giggle.

"We have enough laws," Jim Paulson shouted. "If that's what you're getting at." Frankie and Ty sat in his row, along with Nicole and Tess and a few assorted parents. I didn't see Mario, Nick, or Demitri anywhere.

A ranger, who must be Meredith Taylor, stood from her front row seat. "This is a public forum, and as we mentioned from the start everyone will have a chance to speak. However, we ask that you hold your comments until the end of the presentation."

Jim gave the man sitting next to him a look and folded his arms.

"Who's that guy sitting next to Jim?" I asked Ruth.

"Ty's dad, Mack." Ruth said.

"Shhh," a woman in front of us hissed.

Ruth made a face once the woman turned back around, and I bit my lip. So much boiled up in me, worry about bear hunting starting tomorrow, hope that this meeting would prove to the seventh grade that Frankie was wrong—my family wasn't here to boss anyone around, happiness that Ruth was here with me, worry about Dad's new gun and his plans to go hunting, Mom, Andrew, all of it, fizzed up and threatened to turn into uncontrollable, hysterical giggles. I forced myself to breathe.

"Thank you, Meredith." Dad gripped the podium and continued. "We are fortunate to have Helen Baxter in our community. As a black bear researcher, she has seen many bears in many communities. Tonight, she'll give us the facts about living with bears."

He sat next to Meredith as Helen took the stage. No one applauded.

Instead Mack yelled, "We already know the facts. Bears are pests. Send them back to the wilderness where they belong."

"Mack." Meredith stood again. "Please."

I would have been concerned about Dad, but I happened to glance over at Mom, whose face was about-to-pass-out white. It was too stuffy in here. I took her hand, whispered, "Mom, do you need to go?"

"No, I want to be here. For your dad."

Her eyes weren't dilated. She even managed a smile, so maybe she was all right. And even if she wasn't, she was too stubborn to listen to me.

Ruth frowned, her silent question clear. *Is your mom all right?* I nodded because the real answer was much to complicated to explain.

Helen stood in front of a chart, which tracked bear feeding patterns. "Bears don't want human contact. This year we have plenty of berries and other foliage, and I have set up alternate feeding stations at my cabin. The bears are well fed, which means they'll avoid your cabins and stores as long as you keep trash contained in bear-proof boxes."

"Excuse me, Meredith." Jim Paulson walked up to the front of the room. "May I have the floor now? She's had her say."

Dad stood, but looked unsure of what to do.

Meredith said, "Helen wasn't—"

But Jim didn't wait for Meredith to finish. "I'm afraid

our scientist is wrong. Just today, while I was working on my ATV, the bear that so-called scientist calls Patch attacked me."

"Attacked you?" Helen repeated.

The room erupted into loud argument. Andrew stood up from his seat in the front row, his forehead creased with worry. Alone behind the podium, Helen faced the waves of anger flooding the room. I was relieved when Dad walked over and whispered in her ear. She nodded, left him there, and sat beside Andrew.

"Just a minute now ..." Meredith joined Dad at the podium. "Jim, that's a serious accusation. What do you mean, Patch attacked you?"

"She came right up to me. Put her nose on my hand. I shouted at her, but she didn't back off. She stomped her paws and huffed, and if I hadn't jumped in the ATV and driven away she would have charged me."

"That's not an attack," Dad said.

"That's a bluff charge." I told Ruth. "Even I know that."

Ruth took my hand in both of hers and squeezed tight.

Mack stood. "Are you kidding me? We're lucky Jim didn't lose his arm."

"Patch wouldn't hurt a flea." An older woman stood up near the back of the room. "She nosed you because she wanted food. She does that to me all the time. I taught her the trick."

"Are you crazy?" Mack asked.

Everyone jumped to their feet, shouting about feeding bears and not feeding bears. Jim Paulson stood inches from

Helen's face and yelled. Dad talked urgently with Meredith. Ruth and I stood, hand in hand, not knowing what to do. Next to Ruth, her dad tried to calm down the people yelling in the back row. Mom held onto her chair, the only person in the room not standing.

I let go of Ruth and took Mom's arm. "Mom, let's go outside for some fresh air."

"I ..." She started to argue but then let Ruth and me help her out to the car.

Mom didn't feel up to driving home, so I helped her into the passenger seat, angled it back, and rolled down the windows. Ruth and I sat on the hood, waiting for our dads. Ruth pointed out constellations here and there, trying, I knew, to keep my mind off the disastrous meeting. In the dark of the forest, the sky teemed with stars. As I stared at the pinpricks of light, the angry noise of the crowd faded into the background. I felt tiny, even invisible. Safe.

Finally, people poured out of the building. Dad was one of the last out, along with Ruth's dad, Meredith, Helen, and Andrew. When they saw us, they hurried over.

"What happened? I saw you leave with Mom, but with everything going on in there ..."

"She's okay. But she wants you to drive her home."

"I'll leave the Jeep here and get it later," Dad said.

"Is there anything I can do to help?" Ruth's dad asked.

"No," Dad answered. "But thank you. Thanks for helping inside too."

I quickly introduced Ruth to Andrew and Helen and

shook Meredith's hand. Then, Ruth gave me a quick hug before she and her dad left. Mom had fallen asleep, and Dad and I didn't talk much on the way home. But when we pulled into our driveway, I had to ask.

"Dad, what will happen to Patch?"

"She's a research bear, radio-collared, so that might help. Tonight the hunters agreed not to shoot any radio-collared bears as long as Helen doesn't collar more bears. But Patch might be different. Mrs. Rose, the woman who has been feeding Patch, created a big problem. Most of the time problem bears are taken out of the wild. Or worse."

"But they wouldn't—"

"I don't know, Sades. Everyone is really worked up. We'll have to wait and see."

"If you reported Jim—"

"Sadie, we've talked about this. We don't know the shooter was Jim.

"*I* know—"

"Sades." Dad's tone was final.

He helped Mom inside. But when I walked into my room I knew I'd never be able to sleep. Outside, the crickets chirped quietly.

"Time for reason eight, Pips." I brought the scrapbook down to the front porch and sat on the steps.

WHY PIPPA REYNOLDS AND SADIE DOUGLAS WILL ALWAYS BE BEST FRIENDS —

REASON 8: WE ARE THE SECRET NAPKIN-NOTE FAIRIES.
AND STILL NOBODY KNOWS.

She'd pasted a napkin in the center of the page. Just like all our napkin notes, she'd written a quote with a red Sharpie:

Happiness is excitement that has found a settling down place. But there is always a little corner that keeps flapping around.
—E.L. Konigsburg, From the Mixed-Up Files of
Mrs. Basil E. Frankweiler.

Next to the napkin was a picture of Pips making her craziest face, with a note written beside—*Just in case you need a happiness kick-start.* I couldn't help but laugh.

Pippa and I had started writing napkin notes in third grade, using quotes from our favorite books and authors. We wrote in plain block capital letters so our handwriting wouldn't give us away. We slipped the notes into lunch boxes and bags for birthdays, for the entire soccer team on important game days, sometimes just for no reason at all.

"If only it were that easy, Pips."

I knew what she'd say. *You will be happy, Sades. Just wait.*

After all the anger and frustration of the day—the week—with Mom upstairs sick, with everyone in town angry with Dad, and Dad himself acting like a hunter, with Patch in trouble and Big Murphy shot, with the entire seventh grade hating me, and with hunting season starting tomorrow, happiness seemed far away. But deep down, I knew Pips was right. I would be excited again. I could still feel Ruth's hug, strong and steady. I did have one new friend. Someday I'd wake up and Owl Creek would be home.

For now, I knew what to do. I found a napkin in the kitchen and went up to my bedroom. When I got online, I found a quote for Pips almost right away. I wrote with a red Sharpie:

> It is a curious thought, but it is only when you see people looking ridiculous that you realize just how much you love them.
> —Agatha Christie

I'd mail it tomorrow. No emails tonight. Pips would understand.

Chapter 10

Vanishing Point

The next morning, shots punctuated the quiet on our drive to school. I shuddered at each one. Wednesday, September tenth, the first day of bear hunting season.

At the red light, Dad turned to me. "Sadie ..."

I wished we could drive into another world. A world with no hunting and no sick Mom and no Frankie. I had no idea what to say. Dad didn't seem to know either.

"Sades, I love you," he finally said.

When we pulled up to school, three fire trucks blocked the front drive, lights flashing. Kids huddled in small groups, watching the fire fighters rush back and forth from their trucks around to the back of the building.

Ruth sat alone on the front steps, biting her lip.

I hurried over. "What happened?"

"The climbing stump, you know, the big one off the

playground? Someone set it on fire, and the entire middle burned out. The firemen think it smoldered all night. This morning, when the teachers arrived, flames shot up toward the other trees out back."

"The fire's out now, right?" I asked.

Ruth sighed. "Yes, Sadie. But we know who started it."

"No, we don't. We know who was on the roof messing with a lighter a few days ago, but anyone could have lit that stump on fire."

"But Mario, Nick, and Demitri weren't at last night's meeting." Ruth rubbed her hands over her face, across her jeans, smoothed her hair. "That can't be a coincidence."

"Ruth, you worry too much."

"They'll ask if anyone knows anything. We can't pretend we don't."

Behind us, a voice hissed, "If you say anything, Ruth, about anyone, you'll get it from me."

We whirled around to face Frankie, Tess, and Nicole.

"That goes for you too, Zitzie," Tess said.

The day had been miserable. The firemen spent two hours explaining the dangers of fire in an all-school assembly. When your body is one big mosquito bite, the only thing worse than trying to sleep is trying to sit still in an all-school assembly. And Ruth was right. Our principal, Mr. Garrett, announced that anyone who withheld information would be suspended along with those who'd set the fire. Ruth wore her I-might-cry-any-minute look all day. From her seat behind me, Frankie kicked my calf at least ten times.

By the time I got to Vivian's house, my head ached, my calf throbbed, my skin felt like it might burst into itchy flame, and I wanted to scream. Perched on my stool at the art table, I scowled at my drawing of that day's object, a teapot.

"It still looks flat." I scrubbed my eraser across the page.

Vivian came around the table to watch over my shoulder. "Where is your vanishing point?"

I jabbed my pencil at the black grid I had drawn over my picture, lines that were supposed to help me make my object appear three dimensional, as though it vanished right in the center of the page. "It used to be there."

"Sadie, put down your pencil before you poke out your eye." Vivian opened the french doors. "Let's go outside."

I followed her out to the back porch steps, and we sat down, leaning against the railing. Clouds drifted lazily over the treetops, a slideshow of changing pictures.

"Why are you frustrated?" Vivian asked.

"I want my drawings to work."

"You're learning to see in a new way, Sadie. Your brain is screaming, *NO! That vanishing point goes against everything I believe.* But I'm positive you can do this."

"I'm not." I plucked a handful of grass and shredded the blades one by one.

Vivian laughed. "It's not easy to learn something you've always known how to do. You've doodled with crayons since you were a toddler, so you should already know how to draw, right?"

"It's humiliating." I tossed the grass onto the ground.

"Who's watching? Only me, and I know how hard it is. I'm not laughing."

"It's a waste of time, drawing pictures I'd never show anyone."

"What else should you be doing?" Vivian said. "Time is only wasted when you'd rather spend it on something else."

"Well, I ... feel so itchy all the time, not from the mosquito bites, but like I want to crawl out of my skin and start all over again. Nothing fits right since we moved here. I feel like a different person than I used to be."

Vivian nodded and looked up at the clouds. I liked the way Vivian never rushed me. She wasn't like other teachers I'd had, quick to answer. She gave me time to think, to decide if I'd finished my thought or if I had more to say. She treated my words as though each was important, as though each had depth and weight.

"Do you think," she asked after a few more moments, "that *you* are different, or the way others see you is different?"

"What do you mean?"

"Just now, inside, when you drew what you thought you saw, everything was out of proportion. Could it be that people see you as the mediator's kid, someone from outside who thinks she knows it all? Is it all out of proportion?"

"Well, yeah, it's out of proportion. Frankie thinks I'm sneaking around spying for my evil Dad who is plotting to bury Owl Creek in new laws."

"Are you really this upset because of what Frankie thinks of you?" Vivian asked. "People must have misunderstood you in California sometimes too."

"This feels different. I feel different."

"You mean you're changing because of the way people see you?"

"Not into a sneak," I said quickly.

"But you're changing?"

Was I? I'd been quick to rationalize not telling about Frankie and the boys and the lighter, but I'd been furious with Dad for not reporting Jim. I wanted to be the kind of person who did the right thing. Back home, doing the right thing had felt easy. But in Owl Creek, I wasn't sure what the right thing was.

A thought flickered at the edge of my mind, clear, but also difficult to define. "Maybe the right thing's the vanishing point."

I stood, walked back inside and turned to a fresh page in my sketchbook. Back to the teapot. I sketched it again and this time the vanishing point was a little more obvious. At least my teapot looked slightly three-dimensional. Not totally proportional, but close. I promised Vivian I'd draw something with a vanishing point each day this week.

Peter offered to take me home on his way to town, and on the drive he rolled down the truck windows, letting the cool autumn air blow in. For the first time that day, I didn't hear shots. Maybe the hunters had finished for the day. Signs for pumpkins and corn and squash lined the road.

Peter breathed deep. "Fall is in the air. Soon the leaves will start to change." He smiled at me. "Mom doesn't usually get so excited about teaching. You must be good."

I shook my head. "More like I'm a challenge."

Peter laughed. "Well, she likes those too. I'm her biggest challenge so far. Someday I'm going to make something of myself—make her proud. Just as soon as I figure out what I want to be when I grow up."

Peter must have sensed my unasked question. "Oh, I'm ancient—almost twenty-five. I'll get a job one of these days. I trained to be a firefighter until Dad's accident, and then after ..." He shrugged. "Well, I didn't want to leave Mom alone, and honestly, I'm not sure I want to be the first one at a tragic scene."

Peter turned down my road. "Anyway ... my point is Mom loves teaching you, and anything that brings her joy, well, it makes me happy too."

"She's a good teacher," I said. My words seemed a lame response to everything he'd said, but I hadn't heard about his dad's accident before now. I didn't want to pry.

"What did Mom teach you today?" Peter asked.

"The right thing's the vanishing point," I said, speaking aloud the words that had continued to echo in my mind, trying to make sense of themselves. Sometimes life felt like a big game of chance—you might choose right and you might choose wrong, and you'd never know until after you chose. Was that why Dad didn't report Jim? Was I just as bad for not reporting the boys? If the right choice was always invisible, how were you ever supposed to know what to do?

Peter pulled into my driveway. "Intriguing. What does she mean?"

Before I opened my door, I tried to explain. "The vanishing point is the spot in the distance where what you see gets so small, it seems to disappear. Ask your mom to show you — it's kind of crazy when you start to see it. When the right thing is difficult to figure out, it's almost invisible. But maybe you can find it in the end?"

"Hopefully so." Peter smiled at me. "If I figure it out, I'll let you know!"

I jumped down from the truck and waved as he drove away.

From: Sadie Douglas
To: Pippa Reynolds, Juliet Chance, Alice Cheng, Brianna Ingles
Date: Wednesday, September 10, 7:55 PM
Subject: Lip Synch

I'm so jealous. Your lip synch will be amazing. And using black light will be so so cool. I miss you all a LOT.

Yes. I honestly love the forest, even with the bugs. I saw a porcupine today on my bike ride to art class. Turns out they really do have prickles all over them. Don't worry, I didn't get too close. :)

Hunting season started today. I'm trying not to think about the bears running for their lives. Do you think they cringe every time they hear a shot too? Dad says I need to take it less personally. Right.

Send me a video of the lip synch. I'll send you a picture of me disguised as a giant mosquito bite.

From: Sadie Douglas
To: Pippa Reynolds
Date: Wednesday, September 10, 8:15 PM
Subject: Re: Where R U????!?

Sorry, Pips. I didn't mean to fall off the edge of the earth. I read reason eight yesterday, and your picture made me bust out laughing. Ha!

I saw Andrew at the DNR meeting, but only from across the room. I still don't think he's a crush. What about you? Ryan? New boy? Keep me posted, Pips.

I've never seen a book of prayers. What's it like? Are there certain words you're supposed to say? Does it make you feel like you're really praying? I didn't know your grandma was so religious. Do your parents know you pray sometimes? Do they ever pray? Sorry for all the questions, but I'm really curious. I've never thought about God much before. Maybe other people think about him a lot more than I do.

Chapter 11

The Tree House

At school the next morning, Ruth halfheartedly brought up the fire again, but before I could repeat my reasons for not reporting the boys, she said, "Oh never mind, Sadie. Tonight's youth group—you're still coming, right?"

I hadn't asked my parents for permission to go to Ruth's after school, so at lunch I called Mom from the office. The day ended up being almost normal, except for the Zitzie picture that Abby and Erin drew and posted on the white board during recess. Frankie's nickname for me had caught on.

Ruth and I spent the afternoon playing Disneyland with Mark and Hannah, after they learned I'd been to the park not once, but three times. Ruth kept apologizing, but I didn't mind. Her little brother and sister were daredevils, and their trampoline version of Space Mountain was fun, in a say-your-final-prayers kind of way.

Later that evening, Ruth's mom drove us to the church, a small A-frame sanctuary with stained glass windows. Ruth and I waved to her mom, and then wound through the maze of buildings into the woods. Ruth wasn't kidding. Not only did they meet in a tree house—they met in the craziest, rambliest one I'd ever seen. Weathervanes and wind chimes spun and sang on top of randomly placed chimneys and turrets.

Ruth held out the rope ladder. "You first."

"Are you sure it's safe?" I asked.

A young woman's face, topped with black and teal spiky hair, looked down through the hole. "Come on up. We don't bite."

"Are all youth groups like this?" I asked.

"Go!" Ruth said.

I grabbed hold of the rope and climbed. The spiky-haired woman pulled me onto the deck and then helped Ruth.

"Sadie, this is Penny. She's the one who leads our trips."

I tried not to stare. Penny, with her teal hair and ears pierced in five places apiece, didn't look anything like the youth group leader I'd pictured.

"Nice to meet you," Penny said. "Ruth told me you might come tonight. Our other leaders are around here someplace. Ben does all the audio visual stuff—anything with cords—and Doug's in charge of everything else."

Across the deck two girls sat on a bench, watching the band tune guitars and check microphones inside. The shorter one looked over and smiled.

"Hey, Ruth."

"Hey Lindsay, Bea, this is Sadie."

"Hi," they both said in unison, smiling.

I'd almost forgotten what being smiled at felt like. A few more people came up the ladder followed by a man with thick-rimmed glasses and a stubbly beard.

"Time to start. Oh, is this Sadie?" He walked over to us and shook my hand. "Welcome. Nice to meet you. I'm Doug." From the creases at the edges of his eyes, I could tell he laughed a lot.

"Hi," I said, suddenly feeling tongue tied.

Ruth led me inside. A few lamps lit the otherwise dark room, and some colored lights pointed toward the band. The twenty or so kids and adults found beanbags and window seats. Lindsay and Bea looked like the only other seventh grade girls. There were a few younger girls, and six older ones—the oldest looked like a senior in high school. I always had trouble guessing boy's ages, but they were scattered too, a few younger, and more older. No one frowned at me or called me Zitzie, which was a welcome relief. Ruth and I took two beanbags in the middle of the room.

Doug went up front. "Just a few details before Equilibrium plays. Next week we'll meet late down by the big rocks for the star shower. Bring a coat because it'll get cold. Penny's arranging a slide show, so don't forget to send her your mud pictures. We also have a guest here tonight, Ruth's friend, Sadie—welcome, Sadie—and I think that's it for my announcements. Am I forgetting anything?"

A guy who looked like he belonged on the football team called, "Yeah, when's the marshmallow eating contest?"

"Those marshmallows!" Doug said. "I keep forgetting. Next week, I promise."

"Doug's just scared," the guy sitting next to the football player said. "He'll never be able to keep his record."

Doug laughed. "We'll see about that. Okay. Let's kick this off with a prayer."

Everyone closed their eyes. I sank low into my bean-bag and watched Ruth. The first time I'd prayed for Big Murphy, I felt a bit calmer but nothing more. Was I doing something wrong?

Doug started praying. I looked up to see if he was watching me, but no, his eyes were closed too.

"God, we're here. We're open. We want to hear from you. Thank you for being with us, for your whisper in the wind and for your laughter in the river. Thank you for your children, Cameron, T.J., and Ryan, who celebrate you with their gifts. Help us be a blessing to one another. Amen."

A simple drumbeat started and everyone opened their eyes. Ruth's expression had been calm and unreadable during the prayer. Had she felt anything in particular? I could ask her, but asking would feel strange. And what did Doug mean when he said God whispered in the wind and laughed in the river? Cameron's guitar started, and T.J came in with the bass. The drumbeat thumped inside my rib cage and chased out my thoughts.

Then Cameron sang. Ruth fought her smile and glared

at me out of the corner of her eye. Cameron looked over at her a few times as he sang, but I couldn't tell if his glance was different for Ruth than for others in the room. I hoped it was. Ruth and I would definitely have to talk more about Cameron.

I settled in and listened to the words. In the first verse Cameron asked question after question. Surprisingly his questions echoed mine. Does God care about every single thing we do? Does he notice when someone cries? Does he know when someone is sick? In the chorus, Cameron, T.J., and Ryan sang together:

> *Your name is I Am, I Am that I Am*
> *And you are strong enough to hold my questions.*
> *And when I feel I can't stand, you help me up*
> *And we walk hand in hand.*

When the song ended, everyone cheered.

"That was our new one," Cameron said. "Now we'll play some old favorites."

They played four more songs, but I wasn't really listening. *Hand in hand?* They talked about God like they could touch him, like he was something real. To me, God was like fog, something you think is there, but when you move closer, it's gone.

Doug got up after the music. "We've talked a lot about connecting with God, about finding tiny moments of beauty in your life and noticing God with you. Does anyone have examples from this week?"

Lindsay raised her hand. "I saw my new baby niece this weekend. I bounced her on my lap, and she wiggled all over. But then I leaned her back, held her in my arm right here." She ran her fingertips over her lower arm. "She looked into my eyes and suddenly, I felt this tug, like someone telling me to pay attention, to notice that moment. Right then, I knew her and she knew me and we didn't have to say anything at all."

"And that tug, that sharpening of focus, do you think that was God?" Doug asked.

"I do," Lindsay said. "But I can't tell you why."

She seemed so comfortable talking about God, about her questions. I didn't even know where to begin.

Doug said, "It isn't easy, listening for God. But you're all doing a fantastic job. How about you, Jasper?"

Jasper was a smaller boy, probably a sixth grader, sitting in a beanbag at the far left of the room.

"Um ... well, we went fishing last Saturday. The light was super bright on the water, and I thought about that story you told about Moses. So I took off my flip-flops."

People laughed, and then a girl in the back of the room spoke up. "I have a comment."

"What is it, Claudia?"

"I told my parents how you talk about God, and they think you don't take him seriously enough. He's God — the creator of the universe. Doesn't he deserve more respect?"

Murmurs started around the room.

"Now wait a minute, everyone. Claudia brings up an

important point. We have to find the tiny ways to connect with God so we see and appreciate all he does, but we also must remember his glory. He does deserve respect, Claudia. And I think that is what the people in this room aim to give him."

"Well, I don't think joking about flip-flops is very respectful."

"I don't think Jasper was joking." Doug's voice was quiet, calm, and sure.

Claudia pressed her lips together and leaned against the wall. Tension. Even here. Still, Ruth looked calm, as though she'd heard all this before.

"Claudia, remember we all see God differently. We have you to remind us to approach God with awe and reverence. And we have Jasper, who reminds us that sometimes giving God our reverence can be as simple as taking off our flip-flops."

A few more people gave examples—God was in a sunset, in the joy at a birthday party, in the hopeful look on a dad's face as he went out to interview for a new job. I'd never considered any of these "God moments," as Doug called them. But the more he talked, the more I wondered.

"People yearn for something beyond what they know. The exact experience is hard to put into words, but when God reaches out to touch you there's a startling moment when you see both the present moment and feel something beyond—you feel God. Our job is to stay open to these moments, which happen all the time. So this week, watch.

Pay attention. Witness God in your life." Doug stood up and asked us all to stand too.

"God, you showed up tonight. Thank you. Give us wide-open eyes to see you throughout the week. Amen."

And then it was over. Cameron and his friends unplugged their instruments, and Ruth pretended not to watch as we talked with her friends, Bea and Lindsay.

"I hope you'll come back, Sadie," Doug said. "Do you have any questions?"

Questions? I had too many to count. But I didn't know how to ask even one of them. "No. Not really, I guess."

"Okay. Well, if you ever do, I'm here. And so is Penny. And I know Ruth is too."

"Umm, thanks."

He moved on to mingle with the others.

I tried to pay attention to the girls' conversation, but I couldn't focus. I wanted to be alone in my room with my sketchpad, to draw the Tree House and its vanishing point. Was that spot, that exact place that faded away into invisibility, where I'd see God?

Bea touched my arm and I blinked, realizing I'd drifted far away.

"Sadie, are you coming for the star shower next week?" she asked.

"Maybe," I said. "Um, yeah. I think so."

From: Sadie Douglas
To: Pippa Reynolds
Date: Thursday, September 11, 9:20 PM
Subject: Crazy Hair

Don't listen to any of them, Pips. Run your race, and who cares if you beat Ryan. If he's the right kind of guy, he won't be mad. In fact, if he's the right kind of guy, he'll be impressed!!!

One of the youth leaders at the Tree House has black and teal spiky hair. That's weird, isn't it, for a youth leader? But cool too. Would you dye your hair? What color? I think I'd choose purple streaks. But only that spray in and wash out stuff, because what if I hated it? :)

Thanks for answering my prayer questions. I think I'll look for that prayer book at the library. I never know what to say, and the book you recommended sounds helpful. What's it called? I don't think I'll talk to my parents about praying just yet. I want to figure it out for myself first.

As far as I know, Big Murphy and Patch and her cubs are all still okay.

Chapter 12

Perspective

"What's Mom doing in the closet?" I asked Dad when I walked into the kitchen.

Dad wore the Sugar-and-Spice apron and carefully watched a pan of scrambled eggs. "Done!"

I scrambled backward to avoid being smacked in the head with the pan as he whipped around and divvied up the eggs.

"Seriously, Dad, someday you're going to hurt someone."

"Perfect eggs are extremely important." He brought the plates to the table.

"Are you sure you want to interrupt Mom?" I asked as he picked up the third plate. "What's she doing, anyway?"

I'd caught him mouth open, ready to shout. He closed his mouth and winked. "Guess I'd better not. I'll just take them in to her. She's organizing."

Interrupting Mom mid-organization was more dangerous

than Dad frying eggs. I'd had to duck at least ten flying shoes while learning the hard way. But if she was organizing, she must be feeling much better.

I gave him a wink of my own. "Good luck."

"I'll tiptoe. I'll be the invisible man. She won't have the faintest idea I was there."

Thirty seconds after he'd left the kitchen, Mom shouted, "Out! Out! Out!"

After he'd come back to the table, she called, "Thank you!" Humming to himself, Dad dug into his eggs. I'd already eaten half of mine.

"These are good, Dad."

"Good? *Good?*" Dad shouted. "They aren't good. They're excellent. In fact, they're superb."

From down the hall, Mom called, "They're marvelous!"

I grinned and took my last bite. Not even Frankie could ruin a day like today.

But half an hour later, when we pulled up to school, my stomach tightened. Clumps of whispering students shot me dark looks as I walked up the school's front steps. I'd gotten used to the cold shoulder, but this was different. People were truly angry.

As I turned the corner toward our classroom, Ruth collided with me, red-faced and breathless. She pulled me to the side of the corridor and opened her mouth to say something, but just then Tess and Nicole passed by. Tess raised an eyebrow at Ruth, and Ruth shrunk back against the lockers.

Tess tapped my shoulder three times, her sharp fingernail jabbing me deeper each time. I rounded on her. "What?"

"So, yesterday, you went to the principal's office during lunch. Today, Mario, Nick, and Demitri are suspended. How do you think that happened, Sadie?"

I narrowed my eyes. "I was in the office to call my mom, to ask if I could go to Ruth's house after school."

"And to report the boys for starting the fire?" Nicole asked.

I studied the pained expression on Ruth's face. Had she told on the boys? She couldn't believe Tess and Nicole's accusation, not after I'd refused to tell so many times.

Finally I said, "I didn't tell on them." Though it was pointless. If Tess and Nicole had decided I told, nothing I said now would change their minds.

"And even if Sadie did tell, everyone knows Mario, Nick, and Demitri did it," Ruth said. "They weren't at the community meeting the night of the fire."

Ruth was trying, but of everything she could have said, blaming the boys was low on the helpful scale.

"Frankie said we couldn't trust you to keep out of our business." Tess leaned in so close I could smell her wintergreen toothpaste. "Watch your back, Zitzie."

As she and Nicole walked away, I turned to Ruth. "Even if Sadie did tell, Ruth?"

Ruth was small to begin with, but now, with her shoulders slumped and her eyes on the ground, she seemed tiny. "I'm sorry, Sadie."

The bell rang and she walked into the classroom, leaving me in the hallway to wonder whether she meant she was sorry because she had told and let me take the blame, or she was sorry because she thought I had told and didn't know if she could trust me.

I headed into class and curled into my chair, wishing Pippa were here. Pippa would never doubt me, and I would never doubt her.

The day stretched on forever. People treated me like the sludge lining the cafeteria garbage cans. I avoided Ruth. Friends trusted one another—period. And either Ruth didn't trust me, or worse, she had betrayed me and was now letting me take the blame. To believe that, though, meant I didn't trust Ruth. If I could just wait long enough, maybe the truth of what happened would come clear, without some horrible showdown between Ruth and me. An hour before the final bell, I started watching the clock. Fifty-five minutes. Thirty-two minutes. Seventeen minutes. Twelve minutes.

"Before you go," Ms. Barton said, "I want to introduce our word study project. You will each pick a word to investigate. For instance, you might pick the word *dream*."

Abby didn't bother to raise her hand. "What do you mean, investigate a word?"

Ms. Barton opened a blue cloth-covered notebook, searching for a particular page. "I've already begun researching my word, which is *mother*."

She read, "A mother is not a person to lean on but a

person to make leaning unnecessary.' — Dorothy Canfield Fisher."

"Who's that?" Abby again.

"She was an educator and a writer. But that's not the point." Ms. Barton read again from her book, "In the dictionary, the word mother is defined as 'A woman in relation to a child or children to whom she has given birth.' "

"What about mothers who adopt children?" Erin asked. "They're mothers too."

"The dictionary leaves a bit out, doesn't it?" Ms. Barton said. "Words like *dream* and *mother* are hard to define because they represent ideas that can't be summed up in just a few words. The word *truth* is another one. Listen to this quote: 'The truth is more important than the facts,' — Frank Lloyd Wright. And, 'Facts and truth really don't have much to do with each other.' — William Faulkner. What do you think Wright and Faulkner are saying?"

Frankie leaned back in her chair. "They're saying that just because someone was playing with a lighter doesn't mean they set a tree stump on fire."

Ty smirked and added, "Just as an example."

As usual, Ruth raised her hand. Sometimes she just didn't know when to put her head down and stay out of things.

"I think Wright and Faulkner are saying certain things are bigger than facts. A mother is more than the dictionary can describe," Ruth said.

Ms. Barton nodded. "Well put, Ruth. So class, your assignment is to one, choose a word that means something to you. Two, find examples of it in images, quotes, stories, poetry, music, and letters. Collect everything you can for two weeks. And three, create a presentation that includes a written report and a creative oral section. Your presentation must include at least one visual aid. You'll get extra credit for creativity."

"I call *cheese*," said Rickey.

"Clearly," Ms. Barton said, "you'll want to choose a word that provides enough material. Words like *hope* and *dream* will take you further than a word like *cheese*. Monday, bring three words to propose. After I approve one of your words, you can begin your project."

The bell rang and I gathered my things, wondering what word I should choose. *Trust* was the only word that came to mind. I used to think I knew all about trust, but Ruth had shown me I had much more to learn.

From: Sadie Douglas
To: Pippa Reynolds
Date: Friday, September 12, 6:15 PM
Subject: Miss You

After the world's worst day of school, because everyone thinks I told on some boys for setting a fire, I went to the library to pick up the Book of Common Prayer. I love the prayer for the evening (even though it uses old fashioned words like thy).

O Lord, support us all the day long, until the shadows lengthen, and the evening comes, and the busy world is hushed, and the fever of life is over, and our work is done. Then in thy mercy, grant us a safe lodging, and a holy rest, and peace at the last. Amen.

I said the words, out loud, three times, and the strangest thing happened. Even though nothing is better, really, this teeny tiny quiet slipped inside me. Maybe this is what Doug at the Tree House means when he talks about noticing God.

From: Sadie Douglas
To: Pippa Reynolds, Juliet Chance, Alice Cheng, Brianna Ingles
Date: Saturday, September 13, 8:41 PM
Subject: When your mom's in organize mode

1. Do NOT interrupt her when she's organizing shoes. For reasons already established but easily forgotten when you're trying to convince her to take you into town because you're going stir-crazy.
2. Do NOT helpfully throw away the boxes she's left in the hall. As she may plan to use them for her new totally incomprehensible organizing system.
3. Do NOT ask her to explain her system. As she feels it needs no explanation.
4. DO hide out on your super-cool round porch and celebrate because your mom finally feels better, and this new house might just do the trick that no doctor ever could. :)

Miss you all!

From: Sadie Douglas
To: Pippa Reynolds
Date: Sunday, September 14, 7:32 PM
Subject: Murder

Meredith Taylor, Dad's boss at the DNR, expedited Dad's hunting application, so he got his small game hunting license yesterday. Today, he went hunting, even though none of the other hunters would go with him. He didn't shoot anything. I guess he's trying to make the hunters like him so they'll listen to him. He told me he saw a moose, and then got really mad when I asked, "You didn't shoot him, did you?"

I can't picture Dad shooting an animal, even if it is just a squirrel or a rabbit. We're supposed to pick a word for this project at school, a complicated word that we want to understand better. We have to choose three. My three choices are trust, hunting, and murder. I hope Ms. Barton chooses murder so I can do my project on how horrible Dad is being.

Chapter 13

Alive

When I got home from school on Monday, Mom had completely reorganized the kitchen and started on dinner. Chicken breasts defrosted on the counter while she chopped up broccoli.

"Should you slow down, Mom?" I asked. "You've been working non-stop since Saturday."

"Are you offering to help?" She handed me a bag of chocolate chips. "Because the cookie dough in the refrigerator is begging for chocolate chips."

"Mom ..."

"Sadie ..." Her voice was laced with warning.

I sighed and took the cookie dough out of the refrigerator. Just because Mom didn't want me to worry didn't mean I could automatically switch off my feelings.

"How was school today?" Mom doused the chicken with

marinara sauce, sprinkled the red mound with shaved parmesan cheese, shook various spices on top, and put the pan into the oven.

Ruth and I sat together at lunch and suffered through a strained conversation about the word study project, but all the topics that really mattered were off limits. I couldn't see how we could continue being friends without really talking.

Mom still waited for an answer, so I said, "Umm … We started a word study project today. I have to find quotes and stories about the word *alive*."

Ms. Barton had talked me out of my other choices, saying, "Choose a word that you believe in, Sadie, one that inspires you."

Dad pulled up as Mom drained the broccoli, but he still hadn't come inside when I finished setting the table. Something was odd.

I called out the front door, "Dinner's ready."

Dad came in with the tight smile he sometimes got when he was very mad but trying not to show it. More importantly, his eye was ringed with black and purple.

"Dad, what happened?"

"What?" Mom came out of the kitchen with the casserole dish of chicken. "Matthew, what happened to your eye?"

Dad sat at the table. "It's dinner time. Let's eat."

Mom set the dish down and sat beside Dad. "Matthew, you look like you've been in a schoolyard brawl. Sadie and I can't just eat and ignore your eye. Do you need ice?"

Dad took a sip of water and set his glass down very slowly.

I stood at the end of the table and tried not to look at Dad's swollen eye. Black eyes were for punk kids, for mobsters and professional boxers, but not for Dad.

"Sadie, sit down." Dad dished chicken onto each of our plates. "Chicken parmigiana—my favorite."

I sat, but didn't touch my food.

Dad took another bite, but neither Mom nor I moved. Finally, he said, "The story of my eye isn't dinner conversation, Cindy. Can I tell you later?"

"You appear to be the only one who can eat right now," Mom said.

Dad set down his knife and fork. "Mack Jefferson shot his bear today near the research center."

My stomach dropped. Not Patch, please not Patch. And not Big Murphy. Tears spilled down my cheeks. How could the hunters do it? How could they shoot our bears?

"Helen and I helped him pull the bear out from the bush. We needed to know ... We were hoping ..." His voice cracked.

"It was Humphrey," he said finally. "Helen's bear."

"It's not fair!" I pushed my chair back, almost knocking Dad over. "They're *murderers*."

"Sadie, they're hunters. We're not here to stop that," Mom said.

"But I can't believe Dad just lets them—"

Mom's look stopped me. Whatever I thought, she expected me to keep it to myself.

"How did you get your black eye?" Mom took a bite of

chicken and tried too hard to look casual, the same expression she used when she asked me about an unexpectedly low grade.

Dad ran his fingers through his hair. "Mack had a bunch of hunter friends with him. Jim Paulson, for one. When we pulled out Humphrey, Helen cried, and of course Jim started in on her. He was merciless. I lost my temper. And then Helen lost her temper and shoved Jim. He shoved her back, so I got between them, and he punched me. It got out of hand really quickly."

"Matthew, how is this mediating? First, you buy a gun, which I've never wanted in my house. Then, you go out hunting, and now you're punching hunters? This town is changing you."

"I'm not changing, Cindy. I just—"

They both looked over at me, as though they had suddenly remembered I was at the table. I listened to the silence grow and deepen until I thought I might disappear into it. I shoved away from the table and ran upstairs to my bedroom, slamming my door behind me.

I leaned against my door, my parents' words still echoing in my ears. Sick to my stomach, I crawled into bed and pulled the covers up to my chin. I rolled onto one side and the other. I fluffed my pillows. I closed my eyes and counted to fifty, hoping I might fall asleep. I listened to Mom and Dad come upstairs, knock softly on my door, and discuss whether to let me be or come inside. I held my breath until Dad suggested they talk to me tomorrow, until I heard the soft thump of their bedroom door closing. Still, as the quiet settled again, Dad's bruised face swam in front of my eyes. Finally, I threw off my covers. Absolutely, positively time for reason seven.

WHY PIPPA REYNOLDS AND SADIE DOUGLAS WILL ALWAYS BE BEST FRIENDS —

REASON 7: TOGETHER, WE LEARNED THAT A PEANUT BUTTER AND DORITOS SANDWICH CAN FIX ANYTHING.

Pips and I had needed peanut butter and Doritos sandwiches quite a few times. The first time was when my fairy costume had been lost in the mail, the one Pippa and I had carefully planned and both ordered so we'd match. So she had hers in time for Halloween, and I didn't. I'd been in tears, so Mom had turned over the kitchen before taking us trick-or-treating. "We'll make any dinner you want," she'd said. We'd put together the most random combination we could think of — PB and D — and were shocked, and overtaken with giggles, when it turned out to be delicious.

In the picture, Pippa laughed in her Doritos-stained purple fairy dress, and I lay on the floor, breathless with laughter, in my pink tutu with paper fairy wings. All around us, boxes and bags of every ingredient possible crowded the counters. Other photos crammed the pages. Pips and me in front of the soggy refrigerator boxes that had been our fort until her sister turned the hose on them. Pips and me waiting on the bleachers after losing a soccer championship in overtime when a player on our team accidentally kicked the ball into our goal.

My stomach growled. I closed the book and climbed out of bed.

"Well, Pips, I'll try it. I didn't eat dinner tonight anyway."

Thankfully, we had a fresh bag of Doritos and my favorite peanut butter—Skippy, extra crunchy. I made the sandwich and went to the darkened living room to sit by the fireplace. I wasn't allowed to start a fire and figured now wasn't the time to test the rule.

The sandwich tasted like home, but eating it wasn't the same without Pippa. The best part was stacking too many Doritos on top and trying to open our mouths wide enough to take a bite. If our sandwiches fit too easily, we'd make it harder and harder until we made such ridiculous faces we couldn't help but laugh.

"I miss you, Pips," I whispered into the darkness.

I put my dish in the sink and went back upstairs.

On my bedside table I kept a picture of Mom and Dad, arms linked, laughing in front of Yosemite Falls. Mom said Owl Creek was changing Dad, but I didn't want him to change. I wanted him to stay Dad, my laughing, silly Dad who could fix anything.

I brought my drawing pencils and pad back to bed and used the picture to draw Dad's face. I made a shaded box like Vivian had shown me and used my pencils and erasers to draw and redraw until I was satisfied with the shape of his eyes, the curve of his eyebrows, the exact shape of his chin. I began to shade his eye.

So who was Dad changing into? What really happened

with Jim and Mack? Dad stepped between Jim and Helen and got punched—or had he been part of it? Had he shoved or hit someone? What happened after Jim punched him? Had Dad just walked away?

Even worse than the questions about Dad, I realized I didn't know what I would have wanted him to do. So who did that make me? I didn't know Humphrey, but Helen had known him. She'd loved him. What gave the hunters the right to take his life? I wanted to punch Mack in the face. Punch Jim. Punch Frankie and Ty and all the kids at school. My word study word was *alive*. What a joke.

Doug said God connected with us in tiny, beautiful moments. But what about these ugly things? What about black eyes and punching and dead bears? Was God there too? And if he was here, right now, what did he think of me and my terrible thoughts?

I scribbled out my drawing and turned to the next page. The trouble was with the eyes. Dad's real eyes were always full of weather. Either they sparkled with mischief or brooded with frustration, but Dad could never keep emotion out of his eyes. These eyes were the shape and size of Dad's eyes, but they didn't have any life.

Another page. And another page. It didn't matter because I couldn't sleep. I'd draw until I knew every inch and shadow of Dad's face. Maybe in the meantime I'd learn who he really was.

Chapter 14

Light

"Sadie." Dad sat on the bed beside me. "Wake up, Sades. Want to take the day off from school and come to the research cabin?"

I opened my eyes. It was still dark. I'd probably slept only two hours.

Take the day off school? Dad must feel really bad about last night. I shook off my grogginess and tried to figure out what day it was. Tuesday. Yesterday, school had been awful, as usual, so I didn't mind missing more of the same today. If I went to the station, I'd see bears, alive and well, maybe Patch and her cubs, or even Big Murphy. But what if I dissolved into tears over Humphrey the minute I saw a bear? My grief certainly wouldn't help Helen or Andrew. Andrew. In all of my worry about Mom and Dad and Humphrey and Helen, Andrew hadn't crossed my mind. He probably needed a friend right now.

"Sure, I'll go."

The bruise around Dad's eye had green edges. "How long does it take you to get ready nowadays? Used to be you could be out of bed and ready in ten minutes. Remember that?"

For about a month when I was seven, I tried to prove I could read in bed until just before we had to go. Dad had come into my room with the timer morning after morning. The faster I went, the more reading time I'd earn.

"Oh, I can still get ready in ten minutes." I threw off my covers. "Just wait."

He backed up into the hall, smiling. Like always, he was trying to cheer me up, but this time, I wished he would just tell me what was really going on. Was he okay? Was Mom okay?

Dad checked his watch. "It's six forty-five. I'll give you twelve."

When I threw open my closet, I regretted my answer. I wasn't seven anymore, and I wasn't dressing to play in my backyard. I was on my way to see Andrew. Still, a deal was a deal. I tossed jeans and T-shirts across the room, finally deciding on my Yellowstone National Park T-shirt with rhinestones across the front. I dashed into the bathroom, splashed around, and walked into the kitchen at six fifty-five.

"Hey, you did it, with your teeth brushed and all. Nice!" Dad handed me a paper towel with a stack of buttered toast on top, and we hurried out to the Jeep.

As I buckled myself in, I tried not to look at Dad, because even though I had drawn him over and over last night, this morning he looked even more like a stranger.

"We're going to radio-collar April today," Dad said while munching his second slice of toast. "She's one of the other female bears Helen has been watching."

"Can you do that? Isn't that the deal with the hunters — they won't shoot radio-collared bears, and Helen won't collar anyone new?"

"That's why I'm going with her today. She'll need help if anyone confronts her."

I had to bite my tongue before I asked, *Are you planning on another fistfight?*

Dad continued, "I think, and Meredith agrees, that Helen has a good argument for collaring April. After Jim's threats toward Patch, Helen needs a back-up female bear with cubs to research. April will have cubs next year, and Helen can focus on her if anything happens to Patch."

The orange sunrise glow spread into the dark sky. "You can't let Jim hurt Patch."

"Unfortunately, I can't do much to stop him, Sades."

I stared at the toast, completely unable to eat. "What does Meredith say? She's a ranger. Can't she protect radio-collared bears? Plus, Patch has cubs. It's illegal to shoot a bear with cubs, isn't it?"

"Meredith has to answer to the DNR, and the DNR will probably turn their heads if Patch is killed. Jim has reported Patch as a problem bear, and if she survives this hunting season they may remove her from the wild anyway. There will be a lot less red tape if Jim accidentally shoots her."

"But it won't be an accident!"

Dad pulled into Helen's driveway. "Jim will say it was and the DNR won't question him. It's awful, but that's how it is."

"So, that's it? You and Meredith and the entire DNR will turn your backs and let Jim kill Patch?"

"Sades, I'm just helping Helen protect April."

"You should be protecting Patch!" I almost dropped the last three pieces of toast in frustration.

"Sadie, eat."

"I'm not hungry." I handed him another piece as we pulled up to the cabin. The yard was empty of bears.

"I'll eat this one." He jumped down from the Jeep. "But the last two are yours. Remember, Sades, the bears aren't pets. They're wild animals."

Helen walked onto the porch in time to hear Dad's last comment. Her eyes were red and puffy. Still, she gave me her usual smile. "Your dad makes it sound easy. But I happen to know he's desperately in love with Big Murphy. Isn't that so?"

A few seconds later, Andrew rounded the corner, looking tired, but better than I had expected. He carried his usual bag. "Hey, Sadie. No school today?"

Dad swatted a mosquito. "I gave her a pass."

"Did you come to take the puppy home?" Andrew asked.

I looked from Dad to Andrew, and back to Dad again.

Dad laughed. "Sadie was so busy lecturing me about radio collars, I didn't have time to ask her."

"As you can see, the bears are keeping their distance," Helen said. "Ever since we found a stray puppy last Saturday and brought him home."

"Do you want to take him to your house?" Andrew asked.

"What about Mom?" I didn't want to get too excited.

"She'll say puppies are messy and lots of work," Dad said. "And she'll love him."

Andrew grabbed my hand, and suddenly my fingers felt awkward and icy and limp. Before I could figure out what to do, he pulled me toward the cabin. "Come on!"

When he opened the door, a black puppy blinked sleepily, tumbled off the pile of towels he'd been napping on, sat up, and thumped his tail on the floor. When I knelt down to pet his ears, he licked my arms and hands and face.

"We think he's all Lab," Andrew said. "We posted signs, but no one has called to claim him. Check this out." Andrew pulled a dog treat out of his pocket. "Sit!"

The puppy sat and thumped his tail on the floor again. Andrew gave him the treat.

More than anything, I wanted to take this puppy home. I needed someone in my life I could count on. "And I can keep him?" He wriggled onto his tummy, and I scratched him under his chin.

"It sounds like it. Any ideas for a name?" Andrew asked.

"You haven't named him yet?" What *would* I name him?

Dad called in through the open window, "We're heading

out now. Keep a close watch around the cabin for April. If you see her, give us a call."

"Can't we come with you?" I asked.

"The forest is too dangerous with hunters out there shooting."

But not too dangerous for Dad and Helen. Still, it was hard to be mad, with the puppy biting my shoelaces. I picked him up and followed Andrew outside. We sat on the porch steps while they drove away. A rifle cracked deep in the forest and I shivered.

We soon heard a short puff of air. "I wonder who that is?"

We didn't have to wonder long. Big Murphy crashed out of the foliage and headed straight for the window box.

"He's been here one other time this week," Andrew said. "Looks like his leg is healing nicely."

Big Murphy stood steadily on all four legs, ignoring us as he ate.

"He doesn't mind the puppy," I said, as the puppy wriggled and whined.

"That puppy is too brave for his own good." Andrew laughed as Big Murphy lifted his head, huffed, and snuffled his nose back into the seeds. "Want a Sink-the-Boat rematch?"

We wrestled the puppy into his collar and snapped on a leash. On the way down to the river, he weaved in and out between our legs and tangled himself until he was completely stuck.

"He hasn't figured out his leash yet." Andrew carried the puppy the rest of the way to the river.

I tossed a stick into the water and then a rock, which made a good, solid thunk.

"No fair. I've got this monster to deal with." Andrew set the puppy down, but kept hold of the leash.

We launched rocks into the river, hitting the stick until it finally sank.

I sat on a wide rock and pulled the puppy into my lap. "I don't want them to collar April. It's like giving up on Patch."

Andrew threw another stick.

I rolled a rock around in my palm, but couldn't keep my mind off Jim and Big Murphy. "When Big Murphy was shot, we saw someone drive away on an ATV exactly like Jim Paulson's. Dad won't report him because he's not sure."

Andrew pitched a rock at the stick. "But you're sure."

"Well, yeah. Who else would do it?"

"Then you have to tell." Andrew sat beside me. "You could save Patch's life."

"Me? But I meant Dad—"

"He won't tell, Sadie. You know he won't." Andrew leaned forward, his eyes intense. "But you can do it. And you should do it as soon as you can."

I'd pictured Andrew helping me convince Dad to tell, not throwing all the responsibility back on me. How could I tell when Dad wouldn't?

"Sadie, Jim's hunting license would be taken away. Maybe forever, if they can prove he shot Murph out of hunting season. Don't you want that?"

"Yes, I—"

Leaves moved to our left and caused us to come to a complete stop. I scooped up the puppy as a medium-sized black bear loped up the hill.

"That's April. Let's follow her." Andrew took out his phone and texted his mom.

We followed April as closely as we could without spooking her, heading back down the path toward the research facility. Andrew and I stayed back, keeping the puppy as quiet as possible as April ate at the window box feeder. When Helen and Dad returned, Helen pulled on her gloves, slipped the collar over her wrist, took a handful of seeds, and slowly approached April.

While April nuzzled the food in Helen's glove, Helen used her free hand to slip the collar over April's neck and tighten the slack. April shook her head and pawed at the collar. Helen backed away.

"That was so fast. Will the collar bother her?" I asked.

"Not after a while." Helen took off her gloves, as April turned back to the feeder.

I carried the puppy to the Jeep.

"Don't forget, Sadie. As soon as you can." Andrew motioned his head toward the bears before handing me a bag of dog food and another leash. In a louder voice he said, "We got this at Wild Paws downtown. They have a lot more, treats and everything. But this should get you started."

"I hear you're going to a star shower Thursday," Helen called over the Jeep's motor. "Take the puppy. Introduce him to the sky!"

From: Sadie Douglas
To: Pippa Reynolds
Date: September 16, 8:55 PM
Subject: PUPPY!!

I GOT A PUPPY TODAY! I'm not sure what to name him. He's a stray, a Lab, the most adorable puppy in the world. Just like Cocoa.

Pips, I think I have to talk to Ruth tomorrow at school. I waited all day on Friday and Monday for the truth to come out about who told on the boys. Maybe something happened today. But I just can't be friends with someone I don't trust, or who doesn't trust me. I wish you were here.

Chapter 15

Shading

I slid into the seat next to Ruth at lunch. "Are you ready for your report?"

She finished her bite of celery and then said, "Yeah. I'm doing it on *family*."

Maybe I should have decided what to say before I sat down, because now, watching Ruth eat celery, my mind flooded with questions I couldn't ask. *Did you tell on the boys and let me take the blame? Do you really not believe me?*

Before I could sort out my thoughts, Frankie appeared and leaned across our table toward Ruth. "So, I've talked to every single seventh grader, and no one seems to have told on the boys. Sadie here insists she didn't do it, and I'm starting to wonder if she's right. So that leaves one person."

"Leave me alone, Frankie."

"What's the squeaky-clean pastor's kid more likely to do?

113

Tell, because she's so pure and innocent and can't have anything weighing down her conscience? Even when that means letting her new friend take all the blame?"

Ruth ripped the peel off her orange. "Go away, Frankie."

Frankie gave her one last glare and began talking to Ty. As soon as I was sure Frankie was totally preoccupied, I said in a low voice, "Ruth—"

"I suppose you don't want to come to youth group with me tomorrow?"

"I never said ..."

"I thought all this was over." Ruth shoved all of her garbage into her lunch bag and stood up. "I hate being a pastor's kid."

After she walked away, I didn't find another chance to talk to her all day. She hadn't admitted anything, but she hadn't denied Frankie's accusation either. My anger grew all day, anger punctuated by each gunshot that echoed through the woods and into our open classroom window.

By the time I sat down to work in the blue room, anger sizzled out of my fingers. Peter walked into the art studio with a plate of cookies, just as I was busy attacking my page with the graphite stick.

"Woah!" He set the cookies down on the table. "I didn't realize drawing was a contact sport."

"Why am I doing this?" I looked at my blackened fingers and the dark box on my page. "I can't draw over this."

Peter exchanged a look with Vivian before grabbing a cookie. "Later, gators."

As he left, Vivian walked over and stood behind my shoulder. "Maybe you can try again, more lightly. We're going for a light silvery gray."

I drew a new box on fresh paper and tried to rub more lightly. The paper ripped, and I shoved the book away.

Vivian looked me directly in the eyes and then nodded. "Right. We'll do this lesson backward."

"I can't even do it forward."

"Come on," she said. "I've got a surprise for you."

She led me through the kitchen into a small cement-walled room. A pile of brightly colored dishes waited in a stack on the floor. Vivian flipped a switch and the room filled with colored light: red, orange, blue, purple, and yellow.

"What are we doing?" I asked.

Vivian picked up a blue plate. "This isn't exactly an art lesson. But you're in the right mood to help me with my project today."

"Which is?" I asked.

Suddenly Vivian hurled the plate against the wall and it smashed into tiny pieces.

I jumped back, startled. "What are you doing?"

"Feel like breaking some dishes? I need ceramic pieces for my next sculpture." She handed me a green plate with a thick, purple border.

I looked doubtfully at the wall. "I can really throw this?"

"Please do." She tossed another, Frisbee style.

I threw it as hard as I could, throwing not just the plate,

but the entire week, Ruth, Frankie, the ever-present gun-shots, Jim Paulson, Mom's exhaustion, and my enormous questions. As it shattered, something tight inside me loosened and rattled. I couldn't stop. I threw another plate and another, until I doubled over with laughter. Vivian laughed too. Before long, tears streamed down our faces. We threw until two plates were left.

"Ready?" Vivian asked. "Let's do it together, on the count of three. One ... two ... three."

The crash echoed, then gave way to silence, the loud kind, the kind that settles after a fireworks show.

Vivian picked up a few shards and held them under the lights, casting shadows on the floor. "As you shade your drawings, adding light and shadows, that's when your pictures come alive."

There was my word again: *alive*. When every gunshot meant possible death, and suffocating anger met me around every corner, my word felt like a joke. But now, breathless from laughing and breaking plates, and with electricity buzzing in my fingers again—this time joyful energy, energy that made me want to grab a pencil and draw, to rub the puppy's fuzzy ears—I understood why Ms. Barton didn't want me to study words like hunting or murder, or even trust, words that pushed me toward the shadows.

I picked up a shard and held it under the light, looking at the brightest areas, where light gleamed off the shiny ceramic glaze. "You couldn't draw the light areas if you didn't draw the shadowy parts."

"Aha!" Vivian tossed her shard aside and swooped me up into a twirling hug. "You made it an art lesson after all!"

"At least now I won't rip through my paper each time I touch it, right?"

Later, Peter joined me on the porch, whittling a piece of wood as I drew the porch swing, focusing on the light and shadows. Once I had captured the light the way I wanted to, I handed my sketchbook over. "What do you think?"

"Not bad." He held it out, comparing the drawing to the swing itself. "Your drawing looks real enough to start swinging any second."

I took my sketchbook back. "Can I see what you're working on?"

He passed me the little creature, a squirrel with his head tilted as though saying, *Pass the sugar, please.*

"See," I said, grinning at the life-like image. "How can my dad even imagine shooting something this adorable?"

"You mean hunting?" Peter took the squirrel back and used short strokes of his knife to shape the furry tail.

I picked at a loose sliver of wood on the deck. "Dad got a hunting license to be more like the hunters around here, but it won't work. I know it won't. First of all, Dad isn't evil like they are."

Peter put down his knife and looked me in the eye. "Sadie, hunters aren't evil."

"But they shoot living creatures, like your squirrel, and like Big Murphy. They're murderers, Peter."

"Sadie, around here, hunting is a tradition. Almost

everyone hunts." He picked up his squirrel. "I'm making this little guy to commemorate a squirrel I shot this weekend."

As his words sunk in, I stood up to leave. No. I didn't want to hear this.

"Sadie, listen to me." Peter stood to block my path. "My dad taught me to hunt as soon as I was old enough to hold my own shotgun. He taught me the sport, sure, and we eat some of the meat we shoot too, but more importantly, hunting is part of the natural order around here. If people don't kill off enough bear or deer during hunting season, the population soars, and the weakest animals starve to death in the winter."

"Everyone uses that excuse. The bears could find food somewhere. If not here, then they could move on."

"To another community that already has a bear population, Sadie."

"So you shoot bears?" I demanded. "You would shoot Patch, or Humphrey ..." A sob caught in my throat.

Peter put his hands on my shoulders and looked me in the eye. "Sadie, no. I wouldn't shoot one of Helen's research bears. I just want you to understand that hunters aren't evil. The only way your dad will make any progress around here is if people can see both sides of this issue, come to the middle a little more."

His words reminded me of my thoughts about the light and shadows, and also made me long for the electric feeling I'd felt after breaking dishes with Vivian. Why did happiness dissolve so fast?

Peter stepped away from the door. "I don't expect you to see hunting differently this second, Sadie. I'm just asking you to try. Okay?"

I hugged my sketchbook to my chest and nodded. "Okay."

Chapter 16

Layering

I asked Dad to drive me to youth group Thursday night even though Ruth and I didn't talk all day at school. First of all, I had promised to take the puppy to the star shower, and maybe he would magically fix the problem between Ruth and me. I could hope anyway. I brought my sketchbook in case I ended up not wanting to talk to anyone.

Before Dad pulled out of the parking lot, he rolled down the window and called, "Come home with a name. We can't call him the puppy forever."

Ruth stood by the rope ladder with Bea and Lindsay, and followed them when they rushed over.

"Whose puppy is it?" Bea asked.

"Mine," I said. I set him down, and they all crowded around.

"This is the perfect conversation starter, Ruth," Lindsay said. "For Cameron."

"Oh yeah, I think he has a dog too," Bea said.

Ruth's cheeks were the color of tomatoes, but she was trying to smile. I could tell she didn't want Bea or Lindsay to know anything was wrong between the two of us. Her voice was a little choked as she said, "He's adorable, Sadie. What's his name?"

"I need help naming him, actually."

Just then, the puppy sighed and laid his head down on his front paws in such a serious way that we all giggled.

"It's got to be a serious name, like something you'd name your butler. But wiggly too," Bea said.

"Because that's not hard." Lindsay punched Bea in the arm. "Come on, Doug and the guys are having their marshmallow contest while they wait for the sky to get dark."

I let the puppy walk on his leash until he lay down and refused to go farther, then scooped I him up. Bea and Lindsay went up ahead, but Ruth hung back.

"I didn't expect you to come tonight," she said.

"The puppy insisted on seeing the star shower."

"I know we need to talk, Sadie. But can we wait — I mean, until we're not here?" She looked ahead, watching Cameron laughing with his band members.

I nuzzled the puppy's head, breathing in his warm, spicy smell. Whatever Ruth had to say to me, whatever I had to say to her, could wait. In the end, no matter what Ruth said, once we cleared the air, I did want to be her friend.

"So what about Cameron?" I nodded at him. "I've been meaning to ask for more details ever since Black Bear Java."

"He and I have never even really talked," Ruth said.

I stared at her. "How do you know you like him then?"

"Well, we all talk at the Tree House, and when we discuss things he asks real questions, and doesn't expect me or even Doug or Ben or Penny to know the answers. I always feel I should know everything, you know, like everyone expects me to. But I don't think it would be like that with Cameron."

We were close to the rocks now.

"So talk to him tonight, Ruth. See if he'll help name the puppy."

She gave me her best elfish smile. "Maybe I will."

We found a rock and watched the end of the marshmallow contest. The football player, Ted, made it to nine marshmallows. His friend, Leo, got up to eight. But somehow Doug stuffed eleven marshmallows in his mouth all at the same time.

They spit out the goo and used wet wipes on their faces.

"Beat ya," Doug said.

"I'll get you in the end," Ted said.

They all laughed and high-fived each other.

Doug checked the sky. "Almost dark enough. And I see that tonight *Sadie* brought a friend. Who's this?"

"He needs a name," Bea said. "A serious but also wiggly name."

"Which is impossible," Lindsey said. "I've told Bea this."

"Everything is possible," Doug said.

A few people shouted back, "For the one who believes!"

What was this — a church inside joke?

"All right. So your job tonight, as you're watching the mystery and wonder of the stars, is to think about puppy names. That is a God moment if ever I heard of one. The tiniest of beings next to what is almost beyond our imagining." Doug smiled over at me. "As long as Sadie really wants our help."

"Yes. Absolutely," I said.

"Tonight is a quiet kind of night, so I won't do a lot of talking. But talk with one another. Talk about your week and the stars and what you wonder. And listen too."

"Take the puppy and talk to Cameron," I told Ruth. "I'll draw for a little while."

Ruth hesitated.

"Go," I said.

She snuggled the puppy close, and carried him over to Cameron.

I wanted to draw the patch of sky just above the tree line. The trees were a deep black, the sky lighter, and the stars and sliver of moon lighter still. I shaded in layers, working to catch all the shadows.

"You're an artist," Doug said, sitting next to me.

"I'm learning to be."

We sat, me drawing the sky, him watching for shooting stars. He didn't ask questions or push me at all. The longer we sat I felt more and more comfortable, like it really would be okay for me to talk to him.

"I picked up *The Book of Common Prayer* at the library," I said.

"Yeah?" he asked. "What do you think of it?"

"I like it, I think. I never really prayed before, and I don't know what to say."

"The prayers in your book have been prayed for centuries, so they have history and strength. You can almost imagine the voices of all the people who have read them, speaking along with you." He pointed at a shooting star.

I drew a little, thinking, about people praying for so many years. Had they prayed for bears not to be shot? For their parents? For life to make more sense?

"My mom is sick," I said. "Not life and death sick. She has Chronic Fatigue Syndrome. I kind of want to pray for her, but I'm afraid to."

Doug didn't ask why. He nodded and then waited, watching the sky.

"I'm afraid," I finally said, "because what if she doesn't get better? What if my prayers don't work? You always think God is the one thing that's bigger than anything else. Bigger than doctors and wishes and everything. And if God doesn't fix her ..."

"Then no one can," Doug finished my thought. "You know, Sadie, you're right. God doesn't always say yes. Sometimes we pray and things don't turn out the way we want. But praying isn't like wishing. Prayer is about you, not about what you want to happen. Praying is talking to

God—getting close to him. Think of talking to him like you talk to your best friend."

"Like how I tell my best friend about things she can't fix?"

"Yes, like that. She knows how you feel, and you know how she feels, and the space between the two of you gets smaller."

"Does that mean God can't fix things?"

"No. Like I said earlier, with God everything is possible. It's just every single event on Earth affects every other single event. You know, like in the time travel movies, when one chance meeting changes all of history? God sees everything, big and small, and he cares about it all. He wants the best for us." Doug pointed out another shooting star. "Don't try to understand everything all at once, Sadie. Just hang out with the questions."

Ruth came over. "Cameron came up with the perfect name."

"Which is?" I put away my sketchbook and pencils and held the puppy tight.

"Higgins."

"Cameron thinks I should call the puppy Higgins," I called to the group. "Does anyone have other name suggestions?"

Names erupted from the darkness: *Midnight* and *Ranger* and *Pete*.

"Okay, okay!" I laughed, as the real suggestions ran out

and the football players started shouting names like *Rugrat* and *Flea*.

"Should we call you Higgins?" I whispered into the puppy's ear.

He wiggled and sighed.

I hugged him close. "Okay. I'll think about it."

Doug moved over to another group.

I turned to Ruth. "And Cameron? How was that?"

"It's nice to finally talk to him," Ruth said. "I was right. He's different."

I thought about what Doug had said, about every little event affecting every other event. The puppy nipped my finger with his sharp teeth. I rubbed the soft spot on his forehead. "You might be a miracle," I said. Then I tried out the name, "Higgins."

Ruth laid back on the rock next to us, and we looked up just in time to see another shooting star.

From: Sadie Douglas
To: Pippa Reynolds
Date: Thursday, September 18, 10:41 PM
Subject: Higgins it is

Sorry I didn't email yesterday. Even though it's late, I had to email now to tell you we named the puppy Higgins. What do you think?

Do you think people can be friends with God?

From: Sadie Douglas
To: Pippa Reynolds
Date: Friday, September 19, 8:32 PM
Subject: Re: Higgins

Yeah. Maybe you can be as much of a friend with God as you want to. But I'm not sure it's just about what I want. Maybe I'm making it too difficult.

I've been praying the nighttime prayer every night. It helps me go to sleep, even when there is so much to worry about: the bears, Mom and Dad, who hardly talked at dinner tonight. There's another community meeting in a week and a half, but I'm afraid it will be even worse than the last one. Ruth and I were supposed to talk at school today, but people kept interrupting. I'm going to her house after school on Monday. Anyways, FYI, the book is helping.

You finished a whole bucket of red licorice in a week?? I hope the girls helped.

From: Sadie Douglas
To: Pippa Reynolds
Date: Saturday, September 20, 7:01 PM
Subject: Barefoot

I worked all day on my word study report. At first, I thought the word *alive* was just the opposite of dead, but I can't stop thinking about what Peter said, about how weak animals starve to death if no one hunts. A starving animal isn't really alive, not the way I want them to be, anyway.

And what about Mom? Is she alive, even though she's sick all the time?

I looked at reason six as my reward for doing homework all day. How perfect. Yes. Barefoot is best. I went outside and walked barefoot in the pine needles until Mom called me in for dinner.

From: Sadie Douglas
To: Pippa Reynolds, Juliet Chance, Alice Cheng, Brianna Ingles
Date: Sunday, September 21, 8:46 PM
Subject: Arggh!

Higgins has to go out
1. In the middle of the night.
2. In the middle of dinner.
3. Whenever I've just opened a book.
4. As soon as I get into the shower.

You'd think this would be simple, since we live in the forest, but since there are bears and skunks and porcupines, I have to go with him EVERY SINGLE TIME. I promise I'll write more soon.

Chapter 17

Cracks

When I rounded the house on my third lap with Higgins, who had whined and begged all through dinner and now refused to do his business, Mom and Dad's raised voices stopped me a few yards from the front steps.

My whole day had been miserable. Ruth was home sick, so I didn't get to talk to her or go to her house after school, delaying our dreaded conversation yet again. Meanwhile, Frankie, Tess, and Nicole had teased me all day about my "traitor friend" who let me take the blame for her and now was too ashamed to show her face. Even though I tried not to listen, they stirred up my anger, anger at them, at Ruth, at the whole dumb situation.

I lifted Higgins into my arms and edged toward the door, wishing instead that I could run away.

Mom's voice shook with frustration. "You should have told them yourself. But you didn't, so I did."

"I had everything under control," Dad answered.

"Did you, Matthew? This time it was a fist. What if next time it's a gun? These aren't suit and tie guys from Silicon Valley."

"Don't be ridiculous."

"What if they came to the house?" Mom's voice was on the edge of breaking. "What if they came in the middle of the night?"

"Cindy, you'll wear yourself out."

I winced. I knew, from Dad's exhausted voice, he hadn't thought of how his comment would sound to Mom. I leaned against the door, feeling each of Mom's words as she said, "You act as though I'm a glass vase that might break any minute. I'm fine. I'm tired of being on the fringes of everything."

Her voice cracked and my insides cracked along with her. I wanted to shout and scream and kick the door. What good had praying done? She was still sick, hunters were still shooting, and everything with Dad had only gotten worse. Higgins whined and I loosened my grip on him, and then opened the door.

I looked first at Dad, who knelt beside the wingback chair. Mom sat, head leaned back, eyes closed. When I set Higgins down, he bounded over to Dad and wagged his whole body.

We were frozen statues of a family, me standing in the doorway, Dad kneeling, Mom sitting.

"Hey," I said, breaking the awkward silence.

"Sadie ..." Dad said. But right then Mom went to stand up and fell sideways. Dad grabbed her arm. "Let me help you," he said.

"I'm fine!" she said, not too kindly. "I just need to lie down."

She stood, still a bit unsteady, and Dad said, "I'm helping you."

"I'm glad you're back Sadie," Mom said. "Sorry but I'm a bit tired. I'll be back after a nap."

"Sure Mom," I said, and I bent down to pet Higgins to hide my sudden tear-filled eyes. A well of emotion bubbled within me. Dad helped her up to their bedroom, and I closed the front door and then scratched Higgins' tummy when he bounded over to me and wriggled onto his back.

Dad came back downstairs, his footsteps heavy.

"What happened, Dad?" My words were hot, angry needles.

Dad sat back on the bottom step and dropped his head into his hands. "I didn't mean ... It's all ..." He looked up at me and sighed. "Mom emailed Meredith Taylor and told her the true story of my black eye. I shouldn't have lied to Meredith in the first place, but I didn't want her to know about my fight with the hunters."

I hadn't known Dad had lied to Meredith, but it made sense now, how Mom had been more silent each day since Dad got his black eye, more worried. "Is Mom okay?"

Dad nodded and rubbed the bruised edges of his eye. "We'll all be okay, Sadie."

My eyes stung. I felt all shriveled up inside and so very tired. Was this how Mom felt all the time? I picked up Higgins. "I'm going to bed."

Dad stood to let me pass. "Sure, little bug," he said, but even my old nickname didn't make me smile.

I cuddled Higgins against my shoulder as I climbed the stairs and closed my bedroom door quietly behind me. When I deposited him on the floor, he immediately started chasing a dust bunny underneath the bed.

"Pips, reason five better be amazing." I took the scrapbook over to the window seat. I was tempted to climb up to the round porch, but the only way to avoid Mom and Dad was to stay put with the door closed. "I guess we're in for the night, Higgy."

WHY PIPPA REYNOLDS AND SADIE DOUGLAS WILL
ALWAYS BE BEST FRIENDS —

REASON 5: YOU NEVER EVER STOPPED CHEERING FOR ME.
AND I'LL NEVER EVER STOP CHEERING FOR YOU.

Pippa's hand-drawn cartoons melted the lump that had lodged in my throat, and I found myself laughing, and then crying. Pippa learning how to do a one-handed cartwheel, falling over and over. Me playing tennis, hitting the ball up and over the fence time after time. Pippa during her frog-drawing phase. Me learning to dive. All doomed projects from the start. Still, Pippa was right. I truly believed she'd land a one-handed cartwheel and draw a frog that didn't look like a pile of goo someday. She believed I'd learn to keep the tennis ball in the court and soar gracefully off the highest diving board. She'd put a sticky note on this page too.

Nothing is impossible. It just might not be possible yet. -Sadie Douglas.

Higgins bounced into my lap and jumped up to lick my salty cheeks.

"I'm not crazy, Higgy." I pulled him away from my face. "I promise I'm not."

He thumped his tail on the cushion. I wiped my face.

I'd told Pippa that nothing was impossible many, many times. The first time we'd been sitting in the car and blowing bubblegum bubbles. Pippa's just wouldn't bubble.

After ten tries, she kicked the seat in front of her. "This is impossible!!"

Quoting a teacher, I said, "Nothing is impossible. It just might not be possible yet."

Our moms choked back laughter in the front seat.

"What?" I hated being laughed at.

"You just sound so . . ." Mom said.

"Absolutely right," Pippa's mom finished for her.

They told the story whenever they got together. Pippa and I rolled our eyes, but when our moms couldn't hear, we told each other nothing was impossible all the time. And Pippa did learn to blow a bubble — proof that nothing was impossible — even if she tried over four hundred times before she got it. Still, success is success.

I blew my nose, put the scrapbook on the shelf, and turned on my computer.

From: Sadie Douglas
To: Pippa Reynolds
Date: Monday, September 22, 9:45 PM
Subject: Napkin Quote by email

"I know God will not give me more than I can handle. I just wish he didn't trust me so much." — Mother Teresa

Even Mother Teresa had questions, I guess.

From: Sadie Douglas
To: Pippa Reynolds
Date: Tuesday, September 23, 4:45 PM
Subject: Ruth has bronchitis

So she might not be back in school until next week. I don't think I want to go to youth group without her, especially if we haven't talked yet.

Oh, BTW, I LOVED the video of the lip sych. Tell the girls I laughed so hard I did that gaspy thing that Bri makes fun of. I miss you so much.

Chapter 18

Expression

"So what have you been drawing at home?" Vivian handed me a steaming cup of tea.

Back home in California the weather was still hot in the end of September, but today in Michigan, icy wind bit my cheeks every time I stepped outside, and my bike ride up to Vivian's had been the coldest yet. I was glad for the tea.

"I'm working on shading, like you asked ..." I covered my sketchbook protectively, not wanting her to see the many drawings of Dad's eye.

Vivian gave me her now-familiar sharp look. "What's wrong, Sadie?"

I didn't want to talk about Dad or Mom or Ruth or school, and I found myself picking a fight to avoid Vivian's questions. "I'm tired of black and white. I'm tired of drawing porch swings and trees and clouds."

Without thinking, I shoved my sketchbook across the table. Vivian opened it and thumbed through. She paused over the pictures of Dad's face.

Instead of asking how Dad got his black eye, or why I had drawn it a million times, Vivian frowned over my last drawing and then closed the book.

"I see the problem," she said.

"What?" I asked, feeling defensive.

"Faces are difficult, for a number of reasons. But let's start with the eyes. Eyes are where a person's personality shows up most. When I started drawing eyes, I became really frustrated. With eyes it isn't just about drawing shapes." Vivian put a small mirror in front of me. "What do you see in your face right now?"

I glared at my angry reflection.

"Look at the creases around your eyes. Expression is seen in the eyelids and eyebrows."

I made several faces in the mirror. My pupils didn't change at all, but the skin around my eyes folded and wrinkled to show surprise, concern, happiness, sadness.

"That's why shading is so important. You can draw all the shapes you want—the details are in the shading."

I picked up a pencil, suddenly fascinated by my own face. Surprised eyes. Questioning eyes. Suddenly my drawings had life.

Vivian clattered around in the kitchen joking with Peter while I drew. As I listened to them, I started on a set of laughing eyes. The two of them, happy together, reminded me of Mom complimenting Dad on his crazy scrambled eggs. Why couldn't we be like that all the time?

After I finished my drawing, Peter presented me with a whipped cream topped mug. "I call this delectable creation Double-Decker Chocolate on a Cloud. I put whipped cream on the bottom, then added melted chocolate, then milk, cinnamon and nutmeg. I topped it off with more whipped cream."

I took a sip. "Delicious!"

Vivian called from the kitchen. "Sadie, we should probably call your parents. It's after seven o' clock. If you want, you can eat here and then we'll drive you home. We're on our way to Compline tonight, so it wouldn't be an extra trip."

"What's Compline?" I asked Peter.

Peter sat across from me and examined my drawings. "You would love Compline, Sadie. They turn off all the lights at the Catholic church and light the candles. The choir sings gorgeous Latin chants that make you feel like you're swimming in music. I don't go to any other kind of church."

I thought about swimming in music as I sipped my hot chocolate and went to call Dad. He was clearly distracted by Higgins. Dad had always wanted a puppy too.

"Just don't teach him any bad habits, Dad."

"Nope. Absolutely not."

Vivian handed me plates of macaroni and cheese to set on the kitchen table and passed out bowls of tomato soup.

Peter took his last sip of hot chocolate. "Like Dad always said, dessert should always come first."

I put my empty mug in the sink and sat at the table. The soup steam warmed my nose. Every time I talked to Peter, I liked him more. Something sad had happened to his dad, but he didn't avoid the subject, the way I would have. He hadn't avoided telling me he was a hunter, either, or telling me what he thought about my opinions. Alive. The word floated to the front of my mind as I slurped a spoonful of soup. Maybe I could bring Peter as my example for my word study project. Was he so alive, so open, because he had grown up around Vivian? She was the kind of person who turned everything right side up again.

Vivian smiled across the table at me. "I haven't told you about my husband, Sadie, and you've been too polite to ask. He died two years ago. He'd been working on our roof, and he fell."

I opened my mouth but didn't know what to say.

"It's okay, Sadie." Peter put down his fork. "There's nothing to say, really. I used to wonder what would've happened if I had been home helping him repair the leak? But then one day, I realized all that wondering was smothering me, and smothering Mom too. So I stopped wondering. I think that's when I started letting go."

Vivian motioned to my food. "Eat. Or it will get cold."

The mac and cheese was stringy with cheese and topped with crunchy breadcrumbs, delicious, but hard to swallow. Even though Peter had said there was nothing to say, silence didn't seem right either. A question burst out before I could stop it. "Can I come to Compline with you tonight?"

Vivian looked up from her dinner. "You want to go?"

"I think so. No, yes. I mean, yes, I would like to go."

Peter cleared the table. "You'll love it, Sadie."

I called home again, and Dad gave me permission to go downtown with Vivian and Peter. In the truck, Vivian turned on jazz, and we all sat quietly, listening and thinking. As we climbed up the cathedral steps, a sign requested silence as we entered. Stained glass windows lined the building, their colors intense in the candlelight. It was strange, slipping into a church pew in the dark, not greeting anyone. The air was thick with the smell of wax and incense.

Quietly, mysteriously, a song started from the back of the church. Men's voices filled the rafters with words I didn't understand, but which seemed as old, and felt as soothing, as my evening prayer. I leaned back and closed my eyes, letting the harmony wrap around me. I'd thought I'd come to Compline for Vivian, but now, after hearing the music, I wondered if I might come again on my own. When I opened my eyes again, I noticed Vivian sat perfectly straight with her eyes closed, as though the music lifted her up out of her seat. Above us finely detailed paintings filled the ceiling, images of robed people and lions and angels. Their eyes drew my attention. Whoever had painted the church understood how to give eyes the spark of life—people shouting in victory, crying in anguish, dancing with joy.

As the final chord faded, the room grew even more silent,

even more still. No one had shuffled or coughed during the singing, and now everyone in the room held their breath, as if collectively holding on to one last moment of pure joy. The choir broke the silence when they filed out. I followed Vivian, not wanting to talk, not wanting to lose the lingering echo of the music.

From: Sadie Douglas
To: Pippa Reynolds
Date: Tuesday, September 28, 9:00 PM
Subject: Sick

I know it has been days since I emailed. I've been working on my word study project, and then on Friday, Mom got a flu that got out of control. Dad and I have been making tea and chicken soup, but today we had to take her to the emergency room because she was so dehydrated. After she had an IV drip for a couple hours she felt a lot better. The one good part is that Dad has been so worried about Mom, he hasn't had time to worry about the community meeting this Tuesday. All the bears are still okay.

Maybe Ruth will be back at school tomorrow.

Chapter 19

Living and Breathing

I crossed out another day on my calendar. September 29. Twenty-seven more days of hunting season. *Please make it, Patch*, I thought. *Please hide. Go hibernate. Do something. Whatever will keep you away from Jim.*

Dad honked. I grabbed my backpack and hurried downstairs. The tires screeched as Dad pulled out.

"What's the hurry?"

A gunshot echoed and Dad set his jaw. "I have to get to the DNR to prep with Meredith for the meeting tomorrow."

"How can you stand it?" I asked. "Any shot could be Jim shooting Patch."

"Sades, we've talked about this. I can't take sides."

"You're more on Helen's side than on Jim's side," I said.

"That's what everyone thinks, and maybe it's true. I'm supposed to be an unbiased mediator, but instead I've become part of the problem."

He merged onto the main road into town. Another shot echoed outside the Jeep. I stared out the window. Dad *was* part of the problem, making Mom so upset she completely collapsed, trying to be like the hunters with his shotgun and hunting license and then swinging all the way to the other side, getting into fistfights with them. Probably they would purposely search for Patch, even more now, just to get back at Dad. Why, when I needed Dad more than ever, did he have to completely fail me?

When we pulled up to the curb at school, Dad asked, "Sades, are you all right?"

I threw open my door without answering. What could I say? Everything around me is falling apart, and he's mostly to blame? I avoided everyone's eyes and went to the bathroom to avoid talking to anyone before class. Just before the final bell rang, I slipped into the classroom. Ruth sat at her desk, so she must be feeling better.

"Good morning," Ms. Barton said. "It's a big day. Frankie is presenting the first of our word study reports."

Frankie wrote NAIVE in big, bold letters on the whiteboard.

"The word naïve," Frankie said, looking directly at me, "describes innocent, idealistic, unrealistic people. If you're naïve, you don't understand how life works. For my presentation, I've written a short play."

Ty and Nicole joined Frankie. Nicole tied a scarf around her head, pioneer style, turned her back, took a deep theatrical breath, and then spun around, hands clasped. "Oh, Ty, I just have to report them."

"Report who?" Ty sounded only slightly more animated than wood.

"You know," Nicole said. "Those bad kids, the ones who played with fire. I mean, that's dangerous." Here she batted her eyelashes.

"How do you know they are bad kids?" Ty dug his toe into the carpet.

"Bad kids are bad kids."

"That's naïve, Nicole."

"I'm not naive?" Nicole said. Again with the eyelashes. "I'm from Cal-i-forn-i-a."

Ruth winced in my direction as the class burst into laughter and Ms. Barton said, "All right, that's enough. Frankie, I'll speak with you at lunch. Now all of you, sit down."

We spent the rest of the morning completing math proofs while Ms. Barton watched us, looking as though she'd swallowed an angry cat. Her knuckles were white and her eyes flashed, and no one dared to raise a hand, even though most of us had no idea how to complete the math. I finally gave up and took out my sketchbook.

I drew Ms. Barton's eyes first, focusing on the tense lines around the corners. I couldn't see Ruth's eyes, so I moved on to the eyes I most wanted to draw: Frankie's. But my squinty drawings weren't satisfying. *Draw what is there, not what you expect*, Vivian's voice whispered in my ear.

I kept looking over my shoulder to catch Frankie's eyes.

"What are you looking at?" she hissed at me.

I decided I should move on to math. I slid my sketchbook

back into my desk and had just begun to stare at my first proof when the bell rang for lunch.

Since Frankie and her friends were stuck upstairs with Ms. Barton, Ruth and I found a quiet corner in the cafeteria where we could talk. After dreading this conversation for so long, the built-up doom was thick and heavy.

Ruth played with her napkin, ripping little pieces off the corner, and then started to talk. "When Tess and Nicole walked past us in the hall, all of it came back from my first year here. I didn't know what to say, and I ended up saying the very worst thing."

I doodled on the edge of my lunch bag. "All of what?"

"Last year, when Tess found out I was a pastor's kid, she made me her personal challenge. She, Nicole, and Frankie used to invite me over to their houses, where they caked my face with make-up and tried to make me swear. You'd think I would have stopped going, but for the first time in my life, the popular kids had noticed me. Honestly, I didn't care how they treated me." She wadded up her napkin in her fist.

"Ruth—" I put my pencil down.

"Let's just say, when I stopped happily participating in their makeovers, I was deemed unworthy and quickly un-friended. When you came, and we started hanging out, I promised myself I wouldn't let Frankie, Tess, and Nicole ruin our friendship. And then ... I'm so sorry, Sadie."

I couldn't stand dragging this out any longer. "Did you tell on the boys, Ruth?"

"Sadie, they always get away with everything. And this time ..." She unwadded the napkin and smoothed it on the table. "While I waited outside the office for you to call your mom, I overheard Mr. Tyree say that Frankie had reported that Cameron and his bandmates had started the fire. I couldn't let her do that. I just blurted it all out, about the lighters and the boys missing the meeting. I was afraid if I told you, you'd be mad." She looked at me, her eyes watery. "And now ..."

I couldn't keep looking at her. My nose burned, and I was afraid if I started crying, I wouldn't be able to stop. I took a deep breath and poked my lunch bag with my pencil.

"Sadie, please forgive me," Ruth said, her voice quivery.

I pinched my finger and thumb against my nose, where tears threatened. I didn't know how to put this stabbing feeling into words. When I had first met Ruth, I thought someday we could finish one another's sentences, the way Pippa and I did. Now, Pips felt so far away, even though we emailed almost every night. And Ruth didn't trust me, and I couldn't trust her, so how would our friendship ever work?

With my eyes squeezed shut, Peter's words, unbidden, drifted into my mind. *People should try to see both sides, come to the middle a little more.* Even if Ruth would never be like Pippa, I still had to try to see Ruth's side.

I looked up at Ruth. "I will try, Ruth. I promise to try."

Dad waited with Higgins in the parking lot after school. "How was your day?"

I climbed in and Higgins promptly licked my face and

145

thumped his tail on my lap. I scratched his ears, avoiding Dad's eyes.

"It was fine," I lied. "How was yours?"

Dad didn't turn on the Jeep. "Sadie, I'm worried about you. When Mom gets sick, we focus on her so much, but I know this has been a hard transition for you too."

I waited out his intense gaze. "Okay, Sades, you're just as stubborn as I am. But please, if there's anything I can do, tell me. I'm here for you. I hope you know that."

I blinked tears away. Dad wasn't there for me. Not the way he used to be.

"I have good news." Dad turned on the car, and his voice switched to his normal cheer. "Big Murphy settled into his den today."

I didn't want to respond, afraid if I said anything it wouldn't be real.

"Sades, it was so incredible. He dug a hole into the side of a small hill, right underneath a rock, and he's almost closed himself in with dirt and rocks."

"I wish Patch would do the same."

"Patch will wait a little longer. She has to make sure her cubs have eaten enough. All four of them will den together."

Dad turned onto Main Street. "Chinese or pizza?"

"Pizza. And breadsticks."

Higgins thumped his tail, and I clipped his leash onto his collar. "Not for you! For you, a treat from the pet store. If you behave."

I lifted Higgins out of the Jeep and let him pull me down

the sidewalk, his little body bouncing back and forth just like my thoughts.

From: Sadie Douglas
To: Pippa Reynolds
Date: Monday, September 30, 8:22 PM
Subject: Your long-lost friend

Pips, I promise I'm fine. I didn't mean to sound sad. Please don't worry about me.

I wish I could have been there for the slumber party, especially for the midnight hot-tubbing. I miss you. Say hi to the girls.

Chapter 20

Silence

Since Mom didn't feel well enough for the meeting on Tuesday night, Ruth's dad drove Ruth and me, and Higgins, who refused to be left behind, to the ranger station. On the way, Ruth's dad told us about Mark and Hannah's disaster of the day—spilling a full bottle of baby powder on the floor and then blowing it all over the bathroom when they tried to dust bust it up. With Ruth beside me, studying my face every now and then, looking for signs of anger, and Andrew, waiting for me at the meeting, hoping I would report Jim, I appreciated the laughter, even though my stomach muscles ached by the time Ruth's dad pulled into the DNR parking lot.

I held tight to Higgins as we entered the crowd that spilled out the doorway. The building was warm but still the room felt icy. People stood in tense groups, watching the door suspiciously. Meredith bustled around the refreshment table, straightening cups and napkins. She raised an eyebrow at Higgins but didn't say anything. Vivian and Peter waved us over to their seats, so Ruth and I left her dad with a church member and wound through the crowd.

"Sit, Higgins," I said, holding tight to his leash as I set him down on the floor.

Higgins sat politely while I introduced him, but jumped up as soon as Peter stopped scratching his ears. Peter laughed and passed Higgins back to me.

"Ruth, you've met Vivian, and this is her son, Peter."

Ruth shook both their hands. "Sadie can't stop talking about art lessons."

"Nice dog, Zitzie," Frankie said as she brushed past with Ty, Mack, and her dad.

"Zitzie?" asked another familiar voice. Andrew's voice. "Someone's begging for her own spectacular nickname." Andrew smiled at Ruth and knelt down to scratch Higgins' chin. "Hey Ruth. I hear you named the puppy."

"Yeah, Higgins. It was Cameron's idea. From the youth group," I said, nudging Ruth. "In fact, I think I see Cameron over there with his parents."

Ruth nudged me back. "Small world."

Andrew rose and held his hand out to Vivian. "I'm Andrew, by the way."

"I'm Vivian, Sadie's art teacher." She shook his hand. "This is my son, Peter."

As Ruth chatted with Vivian and Peter, my attention

shifted to the front of the room, where Dad rearranged his papers on the podium.

"Where's your mom?" I asked Andrew.

He nodded toward the back doors. "She's standing back there, in case she needs to escape quickly. We hope to avoid a repeat performance of last time."

People settled into seats, and Ruth, Andrew, and I took seats next to Peter and Vivian. Ruth looked over at her dad, who was now surrounded by a small crowd.

"That's the mission team." Ruth grinned at her dad who shrugged and ushered his little flock out the doors onto the front steps. "They're planning a new mission project. He'll be stuck for hours."

For once, Higgins was on his best behavior. He curled up at my feet, sighed, and put his head on his paws.

"So, you going to do it tonight?" Andrew whispered.

"Maybe Dad will."

Andrew opened his mouth, but before he could launch into a lecture, Dad began. "Thank you for coming out on a dark, cold night. As you know, in our past meeting we discussed scientific data about the Owl Creek black bear population. Tonight we'll hear your thoughts and opinions. Each speaker will have the floor, without interruption, for two minutes. When all speakers have finished, I'll lead a short discussion. We'll take all opinions expressed and work up three plans on which you may vote at our next meeting."

"Who will make these plans?" Jim Paulson called.

Meredith stood. "The three plans will summarize the

points of view expressed tonight. The plans will address your varied concerns and will be fair."

Jim snorted and whispered to Mack in a voice loud enough for the whole room to hear, "Fair? We pay extra taxes to bring in a so-called expert. Instead of getting rid of the bear problem, we get a tree-hugging bear lover who makes everything worse."

Ruth grumbled in her seat next to me, "Who's making everything worse?"

Conversations spread across the crowd and the volume continued to rise. Dad leaned in to the microphone.

"You'll all have your chance to speak. Jim, would you like the floor?"

Jim gave Dad a tight-lipped smirk, and walked up to the podium. "I believe in keeping our community safe. I've hunted and killed three bears that terrorized Owl Creek, and I intend to continue. Bears belong in the wilderness outside our town limits. As soon as a bear gets too comfortable here, I say we shoot it. Get them out of our way. No reason to put up with the danger or the peskiness. That's what I think."

Patch. The cubs. I closed my eyes and pictured them in the woods, at the cabin, far from here. *Go hibernate, Patch. You're not safe.*

Dad's face remained expressionless as Jim sat down. How did Dad do that? How, and why for that matter, didn't he simply tell everyone what he knew about Jim?

Instead he asked, "Would anyone else like to share an opinion?"

"Do it now," Andrew whispered.

I shook my head and tried not to look at him.

On my other side, Ruth mouthed, "What?" and I shook my head again.

For the next two hours, townspeople expressed their fear or love of bears. The opinions, placed side by side, reminded me of the light and shadows in my drawings. As the differing views stacked up, played against one another, the argument deepened. With every speaker, I was less sure we'd ever come to a conclusion.

Andrew's fingertips brushed against my clenched fist, and then his hand wrapped around mine. Suddenly, I noticed how loud my breathing sounded, how sweaty my palms felt. *Andrew was holding my hand.* Now, even more than before, I wanted to report Jim, to make Andrew happy, but if I did, after Dad had said he wouldn't, and after Mom reported Dad's fight … what would happen then?

Higgins let out another sigh as Meredith Taylor stood to address the group.

"As Matthew said, we'll create three proposals based on your opinions. After the vote, I hope you'll put aside your differences and support the community decision."

As she said this, she looked pointedly toward the back of the room where Helen leaned against a wall. Andrew let go of my hand as quickly as he'd grabbed it. People started to stand up. I had to say something to him, but I didn't have any words.

Finally, I said, "Your mom didn't say anything tonight."

Andrew's eyes were full of shadows as he said, "Neither did you, Sadie."

"I—"

"I'm going to protect my mom from the crowd." He left before I could answer.

Ruth picked up Higgins and grabbed my elbow, pulling me away from Vivian and Peter. "He held your hand, Sadie."

I took Higgins. Everything was too confused with Ruth, and I couldn't explain what had just happened with Andrew. "You should go say hi to Cameron." I pointed her in his direction.

As soon as she had gone, I scanned the room for Dad. He stood at the podium, watching groups of people talking and arguing. I fought my way to the front.

"Dad, why didn't you say anything? I mean, about Jim?" I demanded, as soon as I'd reached him.

Meredith looked up from gathering cookies and frowned at me.

Dad gathered his papers. "It's not my job to have an opinion."

"It's your job to tell the truth," I said.

Meredith walked over. "Matthew, if you must continue this conversation, please do so at home."

"Dad's not the one talking." I rounded on Meredith. "I am."

Meredith's thin lips tightened. Without looking my way, she said, "Matthew, please don't forget what we spoke about last week. Your job depends on it."

I opened my mouth to speak again, but the look on Dad's face made me close it again. He clamped a strong hand on my shoulder and guided me into the parking lot.

"Stop wiggling, Higgins," I said, much louder than I needed to. And then I couldn't stop myself. "Dad, you know Jim shot Big Murphy, and he's in there acting like a hero. He broke the law, and you're not doing anything at all!"

People turned to look at us. I knew this anger wasn't fair; it was multiplied and quadrupled by the trouble between Andrew and me. If Dad had reported Jim, Andrew wouldn't be so disappointed in me.

I knew I should stop shouting, but I couldn't hold my words back. "You're letting them murder bears because you're too afraid to stand up for what you believe!"

We were almost at the Jeep. Dad stopped and faced me. His forehead pinched together and his eyes were cold as he whispered, "Enough. That's enough, Sadie."

I stepped back from his quiet rage, much worse than any angry shout I'd heard from him before. Without looking back, he climbed into the Jeep. I followed, not sure what else to do, and played with Higgins' velvety ears. I pretended I didn't mind the silence all the way home.

From: Sadie Douglas
To: Pippa Reynolds
Date: Tuesday, October 1, 10:15 PM
Subject: Reason Four

I'm sorry about the race, Pips. That sounds miserable.

I fought with Dad tonight. And I fought with Andrew. And
everything's still weird with Ruth. So I looked at reason four.
I think the scrapbook might be a miracle. I mean, how is it the
right thing at just the right moment? You're right. We are always
closer after every fight. Maybe that will happen with Andrew or
Dad. Or Ruth.

I wonder what happens when you get in a fight with God.

From: Sadie Douglas
To: Pippa Reynolds
Date: Wednesday, October 2, 7:22 PM
Subject: Everyone's sick

Vivian called to cancel lessons today because she had a scratchy
throat and a fever. I'm coughing today too, so Mom is making
me go to bed early.

From: Sadie Douglas
To: Pippa Reynolds
Date: Thursday, October 3, 7:22 PM
Subject: Fighting with God is okay, says Doug

My cough went away, so Mom let me go to the Tree House to-night. It was crazy adventure night, and since leaves have started falling, Penny took us to a grove with piles of leaves and we played King of the Mountain. Higgins loves burrowing. :)

I asked Doug what happens when you fight with God. He said just be honest with God, no matter how you feel. This sounds like another too-easy thing. Until you try it. I tried telling God I was mad. And then I wanted to hide under the bed in case he had something to say back. If I don't wake up tomorrow, you'll know why.

From: Sadie Douglas
To: Pippa Reynolds
Date: Saturday, October 5, 7:15 PM
Subject: Totally Alive

Sorry to have scared you. Besides not talking to Andrew and only fake talking to Ruth, everything is fine here. Even Patch and cubs are still safe. Mom isn't so good. I keep wondering: Why did she and Dad have to get in that dumb fight?

From: Sadie Douglas
To: Pippa Reynolds, Juliet Chance, Alice Cheng, Brianna Ingles
Date: Saturday, October 5, 10:15 PM
Subject: My brilliant puppy

I spent the day teaching Higgins tricks. He can now:
1. Sit. (Only until I step away. Then he goes crazy.)
2. Lay down. (Only if I lay down with him and let him lick my face.)
3. Shake. (If I grab his paw.)
4. Chase his tail. (If I put peanut butter on it.)

Success! Ha!

Chapter 21

Stargazing

I sat at my desk, trying to distract myself with drawings for my word study. Five fifty pm. Andrew and Helen would be here any minute for Sunday night dinner. Dad had invited them earlier this afternoon and then spent the day cleaning so Mom could nap.

When the doorbell rang, I closed my eyes, imagining the argument Andrew and I would have. Mom knocked on my door and I sighed. I couldn't hide in my room all night. I followed Mom downstairs to the front door, feeling another pang of unhappiness as Andrew and Helen came in.

"Matthew promised it was only pizza, no fuss," Helen said. "I invited you all over to the station, but we thought it might be easier here."

Mom took Helen's outstretched hand. "You're our first company. This is perfect."

Andrew followed me into the kitchen to gather knives, forks, and napkins.

As soon as we were out of Dad's earshot, Andrew said, "Listen, Sadie, I'm sorry about..."

I hurried him back out into the living room. "Can we talk about it later?"

When we sat down, Helen and Dad debated when the first snow might be. Mom didn't say much throughout the conversation. She was pale, but her old smile was back.

When the oven dinged, Dad brought the pizza to the table. "Bon Appetit!"

During dinner, no one mentioned bears, the community meeting, the hunters, Dad's job, or Helen's research. Andrew and Helen talked about their favorite hikes in Yosemite, and Dad made comments here and there. I watched to make sure Mom was okay and avoided Andrew's eyes.

Needing to escape, and also remembering poor Higgins on the porch, I said, "Higgins needs a walk."

Andrew leapt out of his seat. "I'll help!"

Perfect.

Dad called after us, "Wear coats. It's cold." Andrew hadn't brought a coat, so I loaned him one of Dad's. I pulled on my red fleece and clipped on Higgins' leash.

The moon was full, and our breath made misty clouds as we walked.

"Is your mom okay?" Andrew asked, glancing back at the house.

I shrugged. "She's had a hard couple weeks."

Higgins darted after a bird and we chased after him.

"How long has she been sick?" Andrew asked.

"Right now it feels like forever," I said. "But it's only been about two years."

I wanted to put off talking about Jim, so I told Andrew about the scavenger hunts Mom used to take me on, and some of our crazy camping adventures. Talking about Mom, the way she used to be, felt hopeful, like one day she'd be that person again. Once Higgins finished his business, we went back to the house, but instead of going inside, I led Andrew up the spiral staircase to the lookout.

"Welcome to my favorite room in the house."

Andrew followed me onto the porch. "I heard the people who built this cabin were really into stargazing. I wonder if there's still a telescope around somewhere."

He yanked open the closet door I thought was painted shut, and sure enough, inside a tarp covered an old metal telescope.

"Want to take it out?" Andrew asked.

I helped him brush off the dust and position the telescope to point at the sky.

He twisted the knobs and squinted through the eyehole. "You've got to see this."

I bent down to look and gasped. Tiny stars, totally invisible to my naked eye, filled the sky. "The Milky Way!"

Higgins barked and I laughed. "Do you want to see too?"

I sat on the floor and gathered Higgins into my arms, snuggling my nose down into his warm fur. There, my face hidden, I finally felt ready to talk to Andrew.

"Andrew, I'm sorry I haven't reported Jim," I said.

"Until Mom told me today, I didn't know your mom was so sick," he said. "I know you want to protect the bears, but I suppose you'd want to protect your mom even more. And making your dad … Anyway, I'm just saying I get it."

"It wasn't really about Mom, I don't think. I just can't … I think I'm afraid."

I braved lifting my head, but kept Higgins in my lap. "What if Patch dies because I'm too afraid?" I asked.

Andrew sat beside me. "Talk to your dad again and see what he thinks. But I was wrong. I shouldn't have told you to report Jim, especially if you don't know for sure he shot Big Murphy. After talking with Mom, I realize falsely reporting him might be a disaster. Let's just keep feeding Patch and her cubs and try to keep her away from Jim."

I studied Andrew's face, taking in his words. Was this what Peter meant about meeting in the middle? Was it possible for someone to believe something so strongly, the way Andrew believed I should tell about Jim, and the way I believed Ruth shouldn't have kept the truth from me, and then truly see the other side? Higgins leapt out of my lap and ran circles around Andrew, barking happily.

"Okay, Higgins," I said. "Time for you to take a look at the stars."

I picked him up and Andrew held the telescope so Higgins could see. Unfortunately, Higgins thought the telescope was a chew toy, not a scientific tool, so he ended up seeing very little of the galaxy. Once we settled him down,

we took turns looking through the scope, naming the constellations until Helen called up that she was leaving.

From: Sadie Douglas
To: Pippa Reynolds
Date: Sunday, October 6, 9:23 PM
Subject: Maybe a crush

I think Andrew might just be a crush after all :) But I mostly want
him to be my friend. He's a really good friend, Pips.

How's your Ryan?

From: Sadie Douglas
To: Pippa Reynolds
Date: Tuesday, October 8, 7:55 PM
Subject: Licorice AND Dr. Pepper?

Ryan sounds like a prince. I miss you, Pips.

Now back to work on my word study project. It's never-ending.
☹

Chapter 22

Texture

"Crosshatching is a way of adding additional color as well as texture." Vivian showed me her crisscrossed lines.

I compared her picture to the tree bark we were replicating.

"What's wrong? You're wrinkling your nose."

I rubbed my nose. "It's just not matching up with what you've said before. You told me to look closely and draw what I see, not what I expect. I don't see any crisscrossed lines on the bark."

"Ah." A wide, satisfied smile crossed Vivian's face. "You've finally arrived at the artist's first question."

"The what?" I dropped my brown pencil. I'd been drawing with Vivian for weeks now, and only now arrived at the first question? How many questions were there?

Vivian took a stack of papers off her bookshelf. The top

one, a reproduction of Van Gogh's *Starry Night*, I'd studied in third grade.

Vivian spread the top three pictures across the table. Next to *Starry Night*, she placed a picture that was mostly green and yellow and red. It was all sharp angles and strange combinations of colors. I could almost make out a face, but not quite.

"That's Picasso's *Woman with Pears*. And this one," Vivian showed me a painting of a girl with a red kerchief tied around her head, "is by Jean-François Millet. *Shepherdess with her Flock*. What do you notice?"

I frowned at the three vastly different pictures. Van Gogh's thick swirls looked more like a complete picture when I squinted my eyes, but still, the image was unrealistic, warped somehow, not what I would truly see if I looked at a nighttime sky. I couldn't find a single pear in Picasso's painting. The shepherdess was more realistic, more like what I'd drawn so far.

"I like the Van Gogh best." I twined my pencil through my fingers. "But it isn't realistic — not like what you've been teaching me to draw."

"So, what is the artist's first question?"

I frowned again, a thousand questions buzzing around my mind, but none that seemed important enough, or clear enough, to be the artist's first question. If artists drew in tons of different styles, why was Vivian forcing me to draw everything realistically? Why were we drawing crosshatching that didn't exist, instead of what we actually saw?

Vivian laughed. "Don't worry, Sadie. When I learned to draw, I wondered all the same things you're probably wondering now." She stood and headed to the door. "To celebrate you stumbling across the artist's first question, let's have tea. See if you can put your question into words when I come back."

While she was gone, I compared the three pictures, so different and yet all intriguing, unique. My mind was a mouse running a maze, finding dead ends around each corner. What I wanted to know was ... I wanted to know...

As Vivian came back, tea tray in hand, a nearby gunshot rattled the windows.

"Why can't they just stop?" I hated the way the shots caught me off-guard, stirring up all my fears. Big Murphy's okay, I reminded myself. Patch will be. Or at least I hoped she would. She'd made it this far. She was close. So close.

Vivian set down the tray. "Why don't you go find a textured object outside to bring in and draw? You can think about the artist's question while you look."

I stood wordlessly as Vivian added cubes of sugar to her tea and stirred.

Outside, I started toward the woods at the back of the house. Cold mist, somewhere between snow and rain, fell. I didn't want to draw bark or another leaf so I scanned the ground for a rock. A motor coughed to life as I rounded the back of the small shed. Peter backed his ATV out of the shed, cut the engine and hurried back inside.

I almost called out to him, but he remerged from the

shed, now wearing a green fisherman's hat with a red feather. I'd seen the hat before somewhere, but not on Peter. My greeting caught in my throat.

He restarted his engine and pulled out. The dented ATV with muddy tires. The red feather flapping on his green hat. My legs went watery. Not Jim Paulson. Peter Harris. Peter Harris, my friend, who had promised he would never shoot one of Helen's bears. He had shot Big Murphy and, like everyone else, he had lied to me. I hugged my arms close, but I couldn't stop shivering.

I forced myself to focus on rocks, to look for texture. Finally, I picked up a rough, triangular stone, flecked with gray and blue and purple. Then, I walked, one foot in front of the other. Once I was inside, I would just draw. Later I would figure out what to do.

As I closed the door, jaw clenched, shoulders tense, I knew I could never hide my feelings from Vivian.

She came into the blue room with a plate of cookies. "Oh good, Sadie. I was about to come find you."

"Why?" I asked. *Slow down, Sadie. Relax.*

I rolled the rock from one hand to the other. I couldn't look at her.

"Sadie, are you cold?" she asked. "What's wrong?"

I closed my fist around the rock.

She sat on a stool beside me. "What is it, Sadie?"

"Peter ..." I couldn't finish my sentence.

Worry faded from Vivian's face. "He was sorry to miss you today."

I lost control of my mouth. I lost control of myself completely. A full-grown tiger sprang to life inside my chest. I leapt off my stool. Listened to my anger humming.

"Peter," I spat each sharp, bitter word, "shot Big Murphy. Before hunting season. He broke the law. And then he told me he would never shoot a research bear. After he already had. He tried to make me see the hunters' point of view."

"He what?" Vivian's face was a mask of confusion.

"The bears already run for their lives forty-six days of the year. It wasn't even time for Big Murphy to run yet."

"Sadie." Vivian stepped closer to me, reached out to touch me. "What do you mean? What happened outside?"

"I thought it was Jim Paulson. Dad wouldn't accuse him because he couldn't prove it. I thought I knew for sure. I saw his ATV driving away. But just now I saw Peter's dented ATV, and the red feather in his hat. He shot Big Murphy."

"But he couldn't—" Vivian said.

"He did. And now that I know it was him, I need to report him."

"Sadie," Vivian moved toward me, eyes pleading. "Talk to Peter. I'm sure he'll tell you ..."

I stepped away and found my back against the wall. "A lie?"

Vivian put her hands on my shoulders. "Sadie, look at me. Peter wouldn't shoot a bear outside of hunting season. He wouldn't shoot a research bear. He just wouldn't."

I felt trapped. I had to get out of there. I didn't know what else to say.

"Sadie," she said.

I ducked away, grabbed my sketchbook, and ran.

"Sadie, wait!"

I yanked open the door, got a running start on my bike, and rode away. I couldn't talk to anyone anymore. I had to be alone.

Chapter 23

Smoothness

The ride home was long and cold, and my fingers ached bone-deep each time I touched my metal brakes. I tried not to stop.

Mom sat in the wingback chair with a cup of tea and a book in her lap, not reading. Higgins lay on her feet. Sometimes I wanted to wrap my arms around her and protect her from everyone, from everything. And just as big a part of me wanted to shout at her. Why couldn't she get better? Why couldn't she be Mom so I could be me?

I made myself a cup of hot chocolate with marshmallows, ignoring my memories of Peter's Double Decker Chocolate on a Cloud. Higgins tried to follow me upstairs, but kept slipping on the steps. Eventually, I carried him up.

I sat in my window seat, breathed in the chocolate steam, and watched my fingers turn redder and redder as they defrosted. My mind flashed from one image to another. Deep indigo Vivian drawing symbols on our whiteboard. Peter whittling the squirrel. Throwing plates with Vivian. Eating mac and cheese. Going to Compline. Patch hiding from Jim in the tree. Big Murphy, injured, crashing through the bushes. The ATV. Dad refusing to report Jim. Peter's hat.

I squeezed my eyes shut, and suddenly, I wanted to pray. Not a scripted prayer from the *Common Prayer* book, but a real conversation with God. I didn't know how. I opened my eyes and scanned my empty bedroom. The emptiness stretched beyond the walls of the room, beyond the walls of my house, making me feel as exposed as if I floated on a glacier, alone on the sea. Was God really here with me? I closed my eyes again, because the emptiness frightened me.

"God," I whispered, waiting, then pushing on. "Doug says you can see our thoughts ... Can you really see all that's happened? I don't know what to do ..."

The clock ticked and I waited, feeling the velvet window seat against my palms, the curtains at my back, Higgins at my feet. I hadn't crumbled to dust, scattered in the wind. Carefully, I opened my eyes, and saw that the dizzy emptiness had shrunk. I hadn't heard any God-like voice or gained any answers about what to do, but somehow God felt a little closer. Maybe it wouldn't be so hard to start whispering to him next time.

Higgins tugged at the hem of my jeans.

"No, Higgy." But I moved down to the floor so he could sit in my lap. I took the scrapbook off my bedside table.

Don't fail me now, Pips.

WHY PIPPA REYNOLDS AND SADIE DOUGLAS WILL
ALWAYS BE BEST FRIENDS—

REASON 3: YOU ALWAYS TELL ME WHEN I HAVE LETTUCE IN MY TEETH,
OR MUD ON MY FACE, OR TP ON MY SHOE.

Pictures of us with lettuce in our teeth, mud on our faces, and TP on our shoes. Pippa could always make me laugh.

"Let's draw, Hig." I brought my pencils and sketchbook to the window seat and shaded my page, laying a foundation for my drawing.

Higgins tried to bite my pencil. Despite his help, I sketched the smooth lines of my window and the wispy snowflakes outside. At first the images laid flat on my page. An extra layer of shading gave them depth and dimension, but I couldn't make my drawing look smooth, the way the windowpanes and snowflakes actually looked. No matter how much I scrubbed and blended, my strokes wouldn't disappear.

A knock on my door brought me back to my bedroom. "Sadie, can I come in?"

No. "Sure."

Mom came in and sat on the bed. "What are you drawing?"

Higgins licked her hands and sniffed her tea, which must be cold by now.

When I didn't answer, Mom reached for my sketchbook. "You're becoming quite an artist."

"Not really. I can't get my shading right."

Mom shook her head. "You're so hard on yourself, Sadie."

"I wish it had worked out better. Us moving here," I said. "You . . ."

She looked me straight in the eyes, her expression free of the usual mask. She let go of our game of pretend and really looked at me, her face full of everything she never said: *I'm sick, Sadie. I'm worried I won't get better. I love you.* And for the tiniest moment, I felt a tug, maybe that tug that Lindsay had talked about. *Notice this. Pay attention to this.* Mom and I were two people, seeing each other. And then it was gone.

She leaned back and her face tightened, "I'm okay, Sadie. Really."

A gaping hole opened inside me, wanting what I'd almost had, wanting not to be shut out, wanting her to tell me she'd get better. Wanting to believe it was true.

"I guess I'll go heat up my tea," she said and drifted out of the room.

I curled up on top of my comforter. I'd wake up when Dad got home.

"Sadie?" Someone called my name and knocked on my door. "Sadie, can't you hear Higgins whining? Come on, Hig, I'll take you outside."

I heard the door open and Higgins' nails click quietly out into the hall.

I cracked open one eye and shut it quickly again against the bright sunrise. My feet felt impossibly heavy and my legs itched. As my mind-fog lifted, I realized I'd fallen asleep in my clothes. I hadn't even taken off my shoes. I sat up, rubbing my face where my cable-knit sweater had pressed into my skin and checked my clock. Seven fifteen, Thursday morning. I went to my calendar and counted days. Nineteen days left of hunting season. Yesterday rushed back—Peter and my argument with Vivian. I threw myself back into bed and covered my head with my pillow.

Dad knocked again. "Sades?"

"Come in," I said.

He took one look at me and burst out laughing. "You look terrible!"

Higgins put his front paws up on the bed, and Dad lifted him the rest of the way up. Immediately, Higgins climbed onto my lap and began licking my face.

"I was going to offer to take you to the research cabin after school today," Dad said. "But maybe you should come home instead and take a nap."

I pushed Higgins off my lap. "No, I want to go."

"Bring your boots then," Dad said. "We might head out into the woods today."

Last night's frozen dew glistened from branches of evergreen trees as we roared into the morning quiet. Dad's country music blasted from the radio. Suddenly, he turned it down.

"Sadie, Vivian called me last night. She's worried about you too."

I froze. I hadn't expected Vivian to call. I wasn't ready to talk about Peter and Big Murphy yet. I tried to change the subject.

"Dad, is Patch okay?"

"I haven't heard a peep from Jim, so he must not have found her."

I twisted the edge of my sweater between my fingers, knowing now was the time. Now. I should tell Dad now about Peter and Big Murphy.

"Sadie, you know I'd love to give Patch a fighting chance to make it through the winter with her cubs. I just can't report Jim if I'm not sure."

I should stop him, tell him. But I couldn't.

God, please help. I'm turning into a very bad person. What am I supposed to do?

Dad filled the silence. "I'm supposed to be standing outside the mess, helping fix it. I can't jump into the middle of it all. Don't you see?"

I didn't trust myself to speak. Dad wasn't making sense. His fading black eye still tinged blue and green proved just how in the middle of it all he was.

"Someday you'll understand," Dad said, as we pulled up to school.

I wrapped my arms around his neck and pulled his rough cheek close. I wanted to tell him I loved him, but I couldn't find words, not even to chase the deep sadness out of his eyes. I let him go and walked to the school steps where Ruth waited.

As soon as she saw me, she burst into nervous chatter about her presentation. One of the first days of school, I remembered feeling like two people, one standing outside myself, calmly observing, and the other very much inside myself, feeling every little stab of pain. Again now, listening to Ruth, I watched from the outside. Anyone watching would believe we were close friends, but I still felt miles away from her on the inside. Why couldn't I just forgive Ruth? Why did the space between us spread wider every day?

"Sadie, are you listening?" Ruth shook my arm.

I forced myself back to the school hallway, away from my thoughts. "I'm sorry, what was the question?"

"Should I say the part about families being like oranges, and everyone being a separate slice?" Her eyebrows scrunched together with worry.

I faked yet another smile. Now was not the time for her to doubt herself. "Ruth, your presentation will be perfect. Don't worry. Do it just the way you practiced."

Chapter 24

Invisible

After school, Dad screeched to a stop at the research station, trying his old tricks to cheer me up.

Andrew threw open the front door. "Where's the fire? Everything okay?"

If only he knew how not okay everything was. I followed Dad and Andrew to the porch, thinking about how merciless Frankie, Nicole, and Tess had been today during Ruth's presentation, and how terrible they were likely to be for mine. I carefully avoided thoughts of Vivian and Peter and what I would say to Andrew about Big Murphy.

As Helen joined us, a gunshot cracked.

Helen winced. "Even though we can't stop the hunters, seeing us out in the forest reminds them of the rules. I still hate it. I hate every second of it."

"I do too," I said.

"You two stick close to the cabin," Helen said to Andrew and me. "Keep the feeders full and don't leave unless you see Patch. If you see her, follow her. Use the transponder if you have to. I don't want her denning somewhere she shouldn't. I know we shouldn't interfere, but …"

She pulled her hat over her ears and turned to Dad. "Meredith is joining us today, which will be a big help."

As they headed off into the woods, Andrew handed me a ten-gallon container of nuts and took one for himself. "You ready to fill the feeders?"

As I poured nuts into the first feeder, they tumbled out too quickly and some spilled on the ground.

"Don't worry about picking them up. The bears will eat them off the ground. They're not picky." Andrew filled the next feeder.

I scanned the bushes, the empty yard. "All the bears are gone."

"Most have chosen dens. Very few are still out, that's all. We're lucky to have only lost Humphrey."

No one had talked about Humphrey since the day after he died. Hearing his name now, added to the weight of what I knew, what I couldn't say, rested on my shoulders and pushed down, down. Maybe if I started by telling Andrew about Ruth, I could figure out a way to tell him about Peter too. Maybe all I needed was to start.

I poured seed into the last feeder and then set my empty container on the deck, sitting beside it. "Ruth and I had a fight."

"Really?" Andrew squatted next to me. "After the meeting? What happened?"

"Actually before the meeting." I looked up at the dark clouds that crowded the sky. "I've been trying to act like everything is okay, but Ruth lied to me, or at least she didn't tell me the truth, and she let me take the blame at school for telling on Ty's friends who got suspended—"

"Woah!" Andrew sat down. "Sounds like a long story."

"She asked me to forgive her, and I'm trying, but ..." I bit my lip. "I don't trust her. How can I be friends with someone I don't trust?"

"Everyone makes mistakes, Sadie. I tried to push you to report Jim, and that was wrong. You forgave me." He leaned down so I couldn't avoid his eyes. "Right?"

Now. Here was the moment again, the perfect moment to tell about Peter and Big Murphy, but when I opened my mouth, I couldn't form the words. Was it because Peter was my friend? Because Vivian was my art teacher? Or simply because all this time I'd been wrong, blaming the wrong person? Was I just too embarrassed now to tell the truth?

Leaves rustled and Andrew squinted into the bushes.

"Sadie, that's Patch and her cubs. We've got to go."

He pulled me to my feet, and we followed the sound into the bushes. We tried to walk quietly, but hiding from Patch was impossible. Either she'd let us follow her or she wouldn't.

"Here, bear," Andrew called quietly into the forest. "Here, Patch. It's just me. Me and Sadie." He continued to call, in the singsong way I'd heard Helen call.

We entered a clearing, and there she was, silent, still, with her three cubs tucked close. She huffed and headed back into the brush. We crept after her.

The cubs bounded around Patch, rushing ahead and then circling back, slipping on wet logs and tumbling into the mud. Whenever they stumbled they stood, shook, and bounded after Patch again.

Finally, when we had come about two miles out from the cabin, and I thought my fingers might actually fall off from the cold, Patch stopped. She stood in front of an embankment held in place with a fallen log. A dinner-plate sized hole had been dug beneath the log and inside the hole a large space had been cleared. A mound of twigs and leaves and dirt stood just outside the opening.

"Her den," Andrew said, his voice barely a whisper. "She's showing us her den."

The three cubs climbed inside, and finally, after giving us a long, long look, Patch squeezed inside as well. Little claws and big claws reached out to pull twigs and dirt back to cover the opening. In just minutes, the den was nearly invisible.

Rain began to fall.

"She's going to be safe." Andrew looked like he could hardly believe his own words. "This part of the forest is an empty lot that has been for sale for years. Out here, no one will disturb her."

"She's going to live," I said.

"She is." Andrew took my icy fingers and rubbed them between his palms. "Let's go back before you freeze to death."

He dropped one hand and texted his mom as we started walking: *Patch and cubs in den. Safe.*

After the triumphant message we raced back through the forest, leaping over logs and charging through puddles. By the time we reached the cabin, rain had soaked through my jeans and boots. Even my socks were wet.

"Where's the den?" Helen called from the porch. From the flush on her face, she must have rushed back as soon as she got the text.

"It's on the open land, Mom," Andrew gasped, trying to catch his breath. "That lot out by Old Man Mueller's cabin that's been for sale for years. She's safe."

I turned circles in the driveway, and Andrew caught my hands and spun me around. Dad grinned ear to ear.

"You'd better take Sadie home," Helen said to Dad. "She's soaked to the skin."

Andrew hugged me tight and then helped me up into the Jeep.

Helen tossed me a towel. "Don't catch cold, kiddo. You and Andrew can show me the den soon."

On the ride home, thunder rumbled in the distance. My happiness started to fade as I wrestled with my growing list of problems — not telling Dad about Peter, not telling Andrew about Peter, what to do about Peter, Vivian, Ruth.

"Looks like a big storm," Dad said, as the wind whipped tree branches into a frenzy. "We should stay in tonight. Hope you didn't want to go to youth group."

The clock read seven thirty. "No, it's too late anyway."

I didn't say that I couldn't face Ruth right now, with the worries piling one on top of the other in my mind. What I needed now was a friend I didn't have to be careful with, a friend I could tell anything and who would help me sort out what to do.

One of Dad's favorite songs started playing, and he turned it up. Now that Patch was in her den, I should be happy. So I sang along with Dad, but every word felt like another stone piling on top of the very heavy pile that threatened to bury me alive.

Chapter 25

Distortion

When we arrived home, the house was dark. Mom must be upstairs, sleeping again. I opened the door and Higgins, who had been just inside, spinning circles, looked up at us. A pool formed under his feet and his ears drooped.

"Oh, Hig," I said. "You've been waiting forever, I'm sure."

The phone rang and Dad went to answer, so I clipped on Higgins' leash and took him outside. After we came back, I cleaned up Higgins' mess. Dad came out of the kitchen.

Something had happened, because Dad, the country rock star, had turned into Dad, the very worried man. Deep lines furrowed between his eyebrows.

"Can you check in on Mom?" he asked, already halfway out the front door. "I have to go back over to the DNR to talk to Meredith."

"What about the storm?" I asked.

Instead of answering, he said, "Eat without me," and shut the door behind him.

I peeked in on Mom, but she was fast asleep, so I made myself a peanut butter and Doritos sandwich and went up to my room. *I'm trying Pips, I really am.*

But even though I was running out of reasons, and even though the reasons were helping less and less, I still needed to look at the scrapbook.

WHY PIPPA REYNOLDS AND SADIE DOUGLAS WILL ALWAYS BE BEST FRIENDS—

REASON 2: BECAUSE WHEN SOMETHING HAPPENS TO ME, THEN IT HAPPENS TO YOU. OR THE OTHER WAY AROUND.

A picture of us smiling, both missing a front tooth. Us, miserable, covered in chicken pox, on side-by-side couches. Us, with tear-stained faces and terrible too-short haircuts.

"But not anymore, Pips," I whispered as I closed the book. "You don't have a huge secret you're keeping from everyone you know. You don't have all these questions with no answers."

Pippa's emailed answers seemed just as easy as they'd ever been, while my questions loomed larger and more difficult than ever. She was so far away—not because she was in California, but because she knew a me that didn't exist anymore. The me who knew what was right and what was wrong. The me who knew what I believed.

My sketchbook was almost full now. I'd drawn as many examples of the word alive as I could. Andrew laughing as he held Higgins up to the telescope. Ruth watching stars with Cameron. Vivan lifting out of her seat at Compline. Dad scambling eggs. Mom in an organizing frenzy. Higgins chasing his tail. Helen slipping the collar over April's neck. Peter presenting me Double Decker Chocolate on a Cloud. How many of these moments were real, though? Which of them could I trust? All around the edges of the pages, sketches of eyes filled the blank space. Ruth's eyes, Frankie's eyes, Vivian's eyes, Peter's eyes, Helen's eyes, Andrew's eyes. Only the last page was empty.

I took out my pencils. Rain pounded on the roof, and I tried not to think about Dad driving through the storm.

I shaded my page with graphite, and then let a shape take form on the page. I was almost finished with both eyes before I realized I was drawing Peter. Not the Peter who shot Big Murphy—the Peter who had lied to me—but the Peter before that, my friend who I trusted. As I shaped and shaded, I realized the two sides of his face weren't symmetrical. One eye stared up at me, hard, cold, from behind a deep shadow, and the other was lighter, warmer.

Finally, Dad's Jeep pulled in. I closed my book and crept toward bed, hoping he'd think I was asleep.

He knocked on my door. "Sadie, you awake?"

I rolled over, turning my back to the door, willing him to go away even as he tiptoed into my room and sat down beside me on the bed.

"Sadie, we need to talk." Dad rubbed my shoulder, as though to wake me, until I turned to face him. "Somehow

Jim Paulson heard that I planned to accuse him of shooting Big Murphy. Maybe you said something at school, or I don't know, Sadie. The point is, Jim stormed into Meredith's office and accused me of spreading lies about him, and then made everything worse by claiming I've been sneaking up behind him when he's closing in for a kill, and shooting into the air to startle his bear. He filed an official report against me for interfering with his hunting."

Even though I wasn't really asleep, I still wasn't following this story. "But you haven't interfered with his hunting."

"No, but I was still called to a hearing tomorrow. It's his word against mine. Sadie," Dad shook his head, "you finally get your chance to share the evidence against Jim. If we prove he did break the law, hopefully the DNR will drop the case against me."

I sat up, realizing what Dad was asking. "You aren't sure Jim shot Big Murphy."

"But I'm pretty sure, Sadie, and you are too. I can't prove it, but if you testify with me we can make a good case."

I lay back down and pulled the covers to my chin. "I can't testify with you, Dad."

Dad laughed. "Sadie, if I had a nickel for every time you've begged me to turn Jim in, I'd be rich. What do you mean you can't testify?"

"I can't, Dad. I just can't."

"What is it, school? You don't want the kids at school to be mad?"

"No, Dad."

"Sadie," Dad said. "If I get convicted of interfering with hunting, I'll get fired. I'll get fined. If they decide to make an example of me, I might even go to jail for a few months. This trial is bigger than whether or not you're popular at school."

The word *popular* prickled along my spine. My sandwich turned to glue in my stomach. I was afraid if I opened my mouth, even to breathe, I'd let it all go. Everything would tumble out of me, word after word after word, and even when the sun came up I'd still be spewing dark anger into the space between us.

"Sadie?"

I swallowed and then carefully strung my words together. "I can't testify."

The words fell like stones into the darkness and anger burned in my throat, ready to pour out.

Dad's voice was steely. "Sadie, you will testify. Get some sleep. The hearing is tomorrow."

He left the room, his legs stiff and mechanical, as though he'd changed from a man into a robot while he sat on my bed. I'd done that. I'd changed him from my soft, loving Dad into something less, something hard and metallic.

His steps echoed down the hall, and he opened the door to their bedroom. As the door shut, I heard Mom's raised voice, Dad's voice answering. I couldn't make out the words, but it didn't matter what they said. If Mom worked herself up, if Dad let her, she'd never get any better.

Shadow monsters reached down to strangle me. My skin burned like I was on fire.

"I can't do this," Mom said, her voice even louder. Loud enough to hear. I didn't want to be part of their argument. I just wanted out.

I didn't wait to hear more. I clipped a leash onto Higgins and ran down the stairs, out the front door, and into the storm. Within minutes my clothes were soaked, and I was grateful for the coolness against my skin. Without the rain, I might burn up into a pile of ashes. Wind roared in my ears, but still I heard whimpering. I picked up Higgins. He licked my face, licked away my tears. I was the one whimpering, not him.

All around me blinding rain fell, making the dark night even darker. Higgins snuggled close to my neck. Lightning lit up the trees and thunder clapped seconds later. I turned, ready to head home, but Mom's voice, her breaking voice, echoed again and again in my ears. I didn't want to go home. I couldn't stand home.

So I turned toward town and ran through the storm, concentrating on keeping Higgins warm. Where would we find a shelter? Who could we ask for help? I traveled on, step after step, mile after mile. I couldn't hear a sound over the wailing wind.

Finally, when I stumbled onto Main Street, lightning flashed again, revealing the buildings dark and closed tight. Higgins shivered, and when I pulled him closer I could tell his paws and ears had lost all warmth. I still felt white-hot, but the tip of my nose was numb, and water dripped from my drenched hair. I tried the library door. Locked.

Vivian had said the Catholic church never locked its doors. They let people in anytime, to sit in the quiet and be still. I splashed through puddles down the block and climbed the church steps. The door creaked open when I pulled the iron ring. I sloshed inside and took off my sweat-shirt to wring it out. Higgins ran circles around my feet, shaking himself off.

When I closed the doors, they muffled the howling wind. Still, my ears rang and I realized I was shivering. I hugged Higgins tight—we both needed to dry off.

I found the women's restroom. Just as I'd hoped, they had a hot air dryer for wet hands. I held my sweatshirt under the air and pressed the button again and again. I took off my wet T-shirt and pulled on the newly dried sweatshirt. Then I pulled off my boots, my socks, and my jeans, and held them under the dryer. The jeans took forever. Finally, when most of the dampness was gone, I slipped them back on and dried my hair. The sanctuary was still and dark, but a few candles flickered on the altar at the front of the church. The air had the same waxy smell touched with spicy incense it had when Peter, Vivian, and I had come to Compline. I chose a pew far from where Vivian and I had sat together and curled up, pulling Higgins close.

All through the drying, my question had grown until it felt as though it would explode out of me. Why was there no one I could ask for help? Why was I here, in the Catholic church in the middle of the night, in the middle of a thun-der storm, alone with my shivering puppy? Now, as I laid my head down on the hard wood in the silent church, I finally realized the truth.

I was alone because I didn't trust anyone. Andrew had said: *Everyone makes mistakes.* My own mistakes seemed the biggest of all. I stood and carried Higgins to the pew in front of the altar and watched the candlelight flicker.

God? I whispered. *I can't do this.* In my words, I heard the echo of Mom's voice, but now, in this quiet room, with the wind howling outside, the memory didn't sting. Mom couldn't make it through sickness on her own. Dad couldn't mediate on his own. Ruth couldn't stand up to Tess, Nicole, and Frankie on her own. Maybe even Peter, with all of his mistakes, had reasons he couldn't admit his fault on his own.

God, please help me.

Warmth spread across my shoulders and down my back. I realized just how tight my muscles had been as my body relaxed. My mind settled too, my worries coming to rest like flakes in a snowglobe, allowing me to see clearly.

I would tell the truth, not so much about who had done what—though I would tell that too. But I would tell the people I loved and the people who loved me how alone I felt. How not alive. I would tell the truth because it was the right thing to do.

As the candle finally flickered out, I curled up on the pew, holding Higgins close, feeling something larger, something I couldn't explain, wrap warm arms around us both.

Thank you.

Chapter 26

Shadows

"Sadie," said a voice. "Sadie, wake up."

Something wet rubbed my nose, and then the inside of my ear.

"I think I saw her eyelids flutter," said another voice.

"It was so cold last night, and if she fell asleep in wet clothes she might have pneumonia by now. She could be in shock."

I wanted to tell them my clothes weren't wet, and I was perfectly warm, but I also wanted to keep my eyes shut—I wasn't ready for the day to begin. I cracked an eye open.

"Sadie," said the first voice again, and now I could see it was Andrew. He slugged my shoulder. "Were you pretending to be asleep? You scared us."

"Go easy on her," Helen said.

Higgins' nose was the wet thing. I peeled him off my head

and struggled to sit up. Bright sunlight streamed through the church windows. My skin still felt warm and tingly.

"Sadie, what are you doing?" Andrew said. "We've all been out since dawn looking for you. People are searching the woods, someone even went out to the Tree House. Mom and I came into town to look in all the buildings, in case you found a way inside. What are you doing sleeping in a church?"

"Give her a chance to wake up, Andrew," Helen said.

I sighed. Telling the truth wasn't as easy as it had sounded last night. "Dad and I argued last night, and I ... needed air."

"In the middle of a storm?" Andrew demanded.

"Andrew." Helen gave him a warning glance. "Sadie, you look like you need a bath, clean clothes, and a hot breakfast. We'll drive you home."

Andrew wrapped his jacket around my shoulders and helped me out to the truck.

Helen flipped her cell phone closed as she slid into the driver's seat. "Okay, everyone knows you're safe."

Andrew didn't pepper me with questions on the way home, which gave me an opportunity to close my eyes and rehearse the day. Dad had said the trial was today. Would I have to go to school? *School.* It was Friday.

"My report is due today," I said as we pulled into my driveway.

"I'm sure you can turn it in another day," Helen said, turning off the station wagon. We waded ankle-deep through the snow to the front door.

"It's a presentation," I said. "I'm supposed to present." My brain felt foggy.

Andrew took Higgins as Dad threw open the door and hugged me so tight he squeezed all the air out of me. He passed me over to Mom, who hugged me and then held me at arms length, as though she wanted to make sure I was all in one piece.

"Let's get you warmed up." Mom led me upstairs to the bathroom.

I appreciated their willingness to wait for answers, though I knew the flood of questions would come later.

Mom set out towels and dry clothes while I watched the hot water creep up the sides of the tub. Downstairs, I heard Dad directing everyone to the kitchen for scrambled eggs. Mom gave me one last hug and closed the bathroom door. I turned the knob off and slipped out of my clothes. My skin was all-over red, and when I stepped into the water it felt like a million bees swarmed and stung me. I closed my eyes against the pain as it worsened and worsened until finally I could feel my toes again. Soap bubbles tickled my nose.

I held on to the all-over-warm feeling from last night. Today—all the questions, the answers—I could handle them because I knew, now, I wasn't alone. Running away hadn't been my smartest decision ever, but I wouldn't trade the feeling—the knowing—I'd had in the church for anything.

The water started to cool off. I got up and wrapped myself in a towel. I pulled a comb through my hair, dried the ends that had gotten wet, and slipped into my jeans and the soft red sweater Mom had laid out.

Bacon and egg wafted up from the kitchen. Food. That was what I needed.

"These eggs are my most spectacular yet." Dad dished up a plateful for me.

"I called the school," Mom said. "They're closed today because the furnace broke."

Andrew grinned at me. "I guess your report will wait until Monday."

"But the trial is this afternoon," Dad said.

I sat down at the table and said quietly, "I'm going to testify."

"Jim Paulson has no idea what he's got coming," Andrew said.

I didn't correct him. I could only stand to tell my story once.

After breakfast, I took a nap until one o'clock. Mom and Dad had already gone over to the DNR, so I rode over in Helen's station wagon with Andrew. I'd insisted on bringing Higgins too. Andrew promised to hold him while I testified if they wouldn't let me take Higgins to the stand.

Instead of a judge, Jim and Dad had to present their case to a panel of people. Meredith was one, as were a few other high-ups from the DNR. A man from the governor's office called the meeting to order and then gave Meredith the floor.

Meredith stood. "As you all know, we hired Matthew

Douglas to help us solve our community disagreements over the bears. As a mediator, Matthew was supposed to remain neutral. Yet, Matthew has had run ins with groups of hunters, and Jim claims Matthew's opinions about the bears have been swayed by Helen Baxter, a local biologist studying our bear population. Therefore, in this hearing, we will not only decide whether to send Matthew Douglas to criminal court for obstructing Department of Natural Resources law, we will also decide whether to remove him from his mediation position."

My stomach, which hadn't been fully calm all morning, started turning somersaults. Dad hadn't been exaggerating about jail and losing his job.

Neither side had attorneys. Jim stood and made his accusations, which were supported by Mack's testimony. Of course.

"And you say you did see Jim shoot Big Murphy?" Meredith asked, turning to Dad. "Please present any evidence that will back up your claim, Matthew."

Dad turned to me. "I'd like to call a witness. Sadie?"

I wobbled to my feet and stumbled up to the stand, clutching Higgins close. He curled up in my lap as I sat and faced the panel of DNR officials.

"Sadie, can you please tell us what you saw when Big Murphy was shot?"

"We heard a gunshot, and Big Murphy ran away, bleeding. Then a man wearing a green fishing hat with a red feather drove away in an ATV just like Jim Paulson's."

Jim leapt to his feet. "She's his daughter. She'd say anything to keep him from going to jail."

"Matthew," Meredith said. "I asked you yesterday, and I'll ask you again now. If you saw this, why didn't you report it to me?"

Before Dad could answer, I looked him in the eye and continued. "I thought it was Jim Paulson, but it wasn't."

On his bench across the room, Andrew leaned forward, disbelief on his face. I closed my eyes, but I couldn't shut out the pain that twisted inside me. No, Andrew, I didn't tell you the truth, even when I really, really should have. Even when I knew, from my trouble with Ruth, exactly how much it hurts when a friend lies.

"Sadie," Dad said, his voice terribly calm. "It wasn't what?"

As I worked up my courage to answer, the doors opened and Peter and Vivian slipped inside, making the worst possible situation worse. So few people had come to witness the trial, and no one had made an official announcement, so I hadn't considered the possibility that Peter or Vivian would show up. They stood in the back, both of their faces difficult to read. Peter's eyebrows pulled together tightly, most likely in anger, and Vivian, her usual happiness entirely missing, pressed her lips together in what I could only guess was disappointment. Disappointment, I was sure, in me. She had asked me to first talk to Peter, and instead, here I was, on the stand, giving evidence against him.

Everyone waited for me to answer Dad's question. In my

lap, Higgins nosed my hand. I put my hand on his warm back, and last night's warmth rushed up my arm, across my shoulders, down into my lungs, unlodging the words I could no longer hold back.

"It wasn't Jim Paulson. I wanted it to be. Jim punched you when you tried to stop the hunters from taunting Helen over Humphrey being shot. Jim scared me half to death that first time I met him, when he shot over our heads to scare Patch. Believing Jim broke the law was easy. But then I saw Peter Harris—

"Wait!" Peter stood at the back of the room.

Why couldn't he just let me tell the story and get it over with?

"Please, listen to me, Sadie." He walked up to the stand and talked directly to me. "I was in the forest with my shotgun, planning my deer hunt, when I turned a corner and walked straight into the biggest bear I have ever seen. The bear stomped and huffed and was so agitated that I panicked. I shot at the bear, and then started running backwards."

I shook my head, not believing his words. If he had shot Big Murphy out of fear, the truth was even more complicated than I had thought. Dad stared at Peter and me open-mouthed.

Peter ignored the whispers of the DNR committee, of Helen, Mom and Andrew, of Jim and Mack, and kept speaking to me. "Sadie, when the bear ran toward me, I thought he was charging. I shot again. Both of my shots hit him in the leg. After it happened, Meredith asked if anyone knew about the bear, and I just … let it go. I was afraid of losing my hunting license."

Meredith scowled at Peter. "This is very serious. You shot a bear out of season and didn't report the incident?"

Peter glanced at Vivian, and then looked down at the floor. "Yes, ma'am." Then, he looked back at me. "I'm sorry, Sadie. The bear wasn't wearing a radio collar, and I didn't know he was a research bear. I would have told you, I promise, had I known."

I traced lines on Higgins' back, because I couldn't look at Peter, or Dad, or even Andrew.

Meredith scanned the room, looking at Dad and Jim Paulson and Peter in turn. "You understand that lying in these proceedings is justification for the DNR revoking your hunting licenses for life? I want you all to think very hard about what you have told us today. Peter, you shot the bear in self defense?"

Peter nodded.

Meredith crossed her arms and turned to Jim, who bit his lip. "Jim, it seems the charges against you have been dropped. Do you still want to press charges against Matthew Douglas?"

Jim Paulson stood slowly. "Well …" He shuffled from foot to foot. "Seeing as how I did punch Matthew the other week, and seeing as how his girl here cleared my name, I suppose I ought to think back, real carefully, and see if it was really him who disrupted my hunting, or if maybe it was someone else."

"Jim," Meredith said, an edge to her voice. "Did someone, or did someone not, disrupt your hunting?"

"Oh someone did, absolutely," Jim said. "Just now that I think about it, I'm not totally sure it was Matthew Douglas. I mean, I never actually saw Matthew Douglas shooting in the air when I was aiming at a bear, when it comes right down to it."

The man from the governor's office stood and gestured to Peter. "You, young man, have some details to discuss with me. As for everyone else," he glanced around the room. "If you straighten out your stories and there is reason for another trial, you know where to reach me."

He picked up his bag, and walked toward a back office. Peter put his hand on my shoulder until I finally had to look up at him. Neither of us said anything, but he smiled sadly before following the man from the governor's office. As he left, I turned to Andrew, passing my sad smile on to him. Every event affected every other event, Vivian had said. Every lie twisted around the last making an impossible knot, but one truth was like a loose thread. When you pulled, the whole mess started unraveling. I looked for her at the back, but she had gone. Just telling the truth didn't erase all the hurt the lies had left behind, no matter how much I wished it could.

Meredith broke the silence. "Well, Matthew, that was embarrassing."

Helen walked to the front. "Meredith, Matthew came here to help us, and we all, including myself, have pushed and pulled him in every direction. The one thing no one has let him do is his job."

"And so ...?" Meredith asked.

"Can you give him another chance?" I surprised myself by asking.

The room went silent, and I wondered into the quiet if Dad deserved another chance, after everything.

Jim cleared his throat, but didn't say anything.

Andrew stood and caught my eye. "Everyone makes mistakes."

"Maybe we haven't given you a fair chance, Matthew," Meredith said. "I'm willing to give you one more meeting."

"I'll give it my best shot." Dad winked at me, a California kind of wink.

From: Sadie Douglas
To: Pippa Reynolds
Date: Saturday, October 12, 8:34 PM
Subject: Re: WRITE BACK

It's such a long story I don't think I can tell it. But it's all okay now. Peter's only losing his hunting license for two years. I'm going to try to draw something for Vivian. I can't go back to art lessons yet, it would be too weird. But I could send her a drawing.

I miss you too, Pips. Maybe you can come visit or I can come there sometime soon. Email just isn't the same.

From: Sadie Douglas
To: Pippa Reynolds
Date: Sunday, October 13, 3:39 PM
Subject: A slumber party and a celebration

April, the very last research bear who hadn't gone into hibernation, has finally gone into her den!!!!! Ruth is going to help me blow up all of the balloons Alice gave me as a moving away gift, and we're going to surprise Andrew and Helen with a celebration. Ruth is spending the night tomorrow night. Things are getting better, Pips! Mom even offered to help with our crazy plan. My presentation is tomorow, and I think I finally got the drawings the way I wanted them. OH! And I sent Vivian the drawing of her sitting at Compline, listening to the music. I hope she likes it.

xo

Chapter 27

Starlight

As I stood in front of the class and clicked on the first image in my PowerPoint, the drawing of Ruth stargazing, I had another moment. *Pay attention. Notice this.* I'd stood here, the first day of school, showing my squat little drawing, and they had mocked me. I'd seen one-toned faces, people to win over. A month and a half later, not much was different between us, but everything was different for me. I was different.

"The definition of the word alive is: *Having life: not dead or inanimate.* At first, I focused on the second part of the definition, not being dead."

I clicked again. Higgins chasing his tail. "I kept thinking about hunting, and dead animals, and how wrong that felt to me."

Next, the picture of Dad with his scrambled eggs. "But

when I started drawing examples of my word, I realized being alive is more about having life, about happiness and fun." I looked up at the image, Mom laughing, so beautiful, the way I wished she could always be.

I clicked one last time, bringing up my last slide, the image I had drawn last night of Helen and Humphrey walking side by side away into the trees.

"Being alive isn't always easy, though. I think being alive, really having life, means risking hurt. Helen gives her whole heart to her research, even though she knows she will lose bears she loves. Being alive means being willing to trust the people you care about, even though you know they will make mistakes, believing that tomorrow they may be stronger or more reliable, or more truthful than they are today."

The bell rang. As people left, I realized Frankie hadn't made any remark at all. Maybe I just hadn't heard it. Or maybe she'd been warned to be on her best behavior. Or maybe, just maybe, now that hunting season was almost over, things would be different.

"Sadie, you didn't tell me about the drawing of me!" Ruth rushed up and threw her arms around me.

"I made you another one, too." I handed her a thank you card. On the front she sat with her cheeks puffed out, blowing into a balloon.

As Ruth studied the image, I grabbed her hand. "Mom's waiting with the balloons in the car. Dad took Helen and Andrew out for ice cream to get them out of the house."

We hurried outside, where Higgins wiggled in Mom's

lap. "Here, Sades, hold him. He wants nothing more than to pop as many balloons as he can sink his teeth into."

The car was stuffed full of garbage bags filled with balloons.

"I owe you, all of you!" I said.

Ruth and I squished in and we sped off to the research cabin. Mom hid the car behind a group of pine trees so we wouldn't ruin the surprise. We hauled the garbage bags inside and attached Higgins' leash to the kitchen table. Then we pushed and shoved and wrangled the slippery balloons between the front door and the inside door so the entire mudroom was filled. Trapped inside now, we strung streamers all around the kitchen. I put the card I'd made on the table.

"They're coming, they're coming!" Ruth called from the window.

I held Higgins up so he could peek with us out the window. Mom knelt down with us as they all piled out of the Jeep. Ruth grabbed my hand and Mom's hand as Andrew and Helen stepped onto the front porch.

Andrew turned the doorknob.

Balloons cascaded onto their heads, rolled across the porch and out onto the lawn.

We ran over to the doorway. "Surprise!!"

"We're celebrating because all the bears are safe!" I said.

Andrew picked a few of the balloons up, and with his very best Andrew smile began pinging them in our direction. Higgins batted at the balloons as they flew over, popping them with his sharp teeth, and Helen ran over to give me a huge hug. Andrew waded through the balloon sea and came into the kitchen. I handed him the card I'd drawn of us watching four sets of claws bury themselves in a snowy den.

We stayed at the research station until dark. After the party had begun to wind down Andrew took us up onto the top deck of the station. The first star of the evening twinkled to life.

"Make a wish," I said.

"I don't know what to wish for after being buried in balloons. Isn't that enough for anyone?"

"Yes," I said. "YES!"

Mom called up, "Time to go, girls."

We took Ruth home and then turned toward our own cabin. Mom and Dad argued over whether to play the country station or the classical. I felt another tug. This moment. Mom, feeling good. Laughing with Dad.

"Thank you," I whispered.

Higgins wiggled in my lap. I couldn't sit still either. It was finally time for reason one.

"Night, Mom. Dad."

"Night, Sades."

I hurried up to my bedroom.

WHY PIPPA REYNOLDS AND SADIE DOUGLAS
WILL ALWAYS BE BEST FRIENDS —

REASON 1: WE'LL ALWAYS BE THERE FOR EACH OTHER
WHEN THINGS ARE REALLY, REALLY GOOD.

Just one picture this time, a picture of Pippa and me, arms around each other, standing on the beach, taken on our last day together back home. Above the picture she'd written, *Happy Adventuring*.

"It *is* an adventure, Pips," I whispered. "A very, very good adventure."

THE END

We want to hear from you. Please send your comments about this book to us in care of zreview@zondervan.com. Thank you.